THE BLUE TRAIN

THE BLUE TRAIN

Lawrence Clark Powell

With an Afterword by Henry Miller

CAPRA PRESS : SANTA BARBARA

Design: Dick Palmer.
Cover: "Gare St. Lazare" by Claude Monet.

The first clothbound edition was printed February 1977
for Capra Press by Mackintosh & Young and R. R.·
Donnelley & Sons. This softbound edition was printed
by the same people in January 1978.

Library of Congress Cataloging in Publication Data

Powell, Lawrence Clark, 1906-
  The Blue Train.

  I. Title.
PZ4.P882Bl (PS3531.0954) 831'.5'2 76-54947
ISBN 0-88496-105-2 (pa.)

CAPRA PRESS
631 State Street
Santa Barbara, California 93101

This is a romance, intended to be to the novel what the string quartet is to the symphony—more compact, chromatic, evocative. It plays variations on a single theme. If it should be thought that actual persons were portrayed, even though it had been so meant there could be little resemblance. Time alters reality, filtering it through memory and imagination, so that what remains is the magic of being young in a foreign land, unburdened by the weight of living that comes later. If Life once sounded discordant, Art has here rendered it harmonious. What then was agitated is now serene. The dedication is to Henry Miller, old friend and encourager.

I

Nancy

On a Friday afternoon of a cloudy day in early November, the wind from the northeast, I stood on the station platform ten minutes before train time, waiting for the 13.36 *rapide* from Paris. I often came to the station late at night when my eyes grew tired from laboratory work, merely to witness the arrival and departure of the express trains that left the capital in the early evening. There was the Blue Train to the Riviera, the Rome, and the Simplon Orient bound for Italy, the Balkans, Athens and Istanbul. For the price of a 50-centime ticket I could gain entry to the platform and watch the trains make their brief stop for servicing.

This time was different. I was bound for Switzerland to what promised to be a romantic rendezvous. I was already excited as I walked up track from under the high ironwork shell that arched over the boarding area to where the freight yards widened out. They were congested and noisy with the crashing of shunted cars. Brakemen were gesticulating and shouting to drivers of the small engines.

The main line was clear, all lights green, the high rails gleaming as I watched for the *rapide* from Paris. Then I heard it approaching, heralded by a shriek of the engine's whistle; and there it was, bearing down with the overpowering majesty of the black and green, copper-banded P.L.M. locomotive, cleaving the confusion of lesser equipment with the authority of the crack flyer, two hundred miles out of Paris, scheduled to pause only long enough to take on coal, water, and passengers.

I stood back and let the long train pass and then halt with a sigh of relaxing air brakes, before I followed it back into the station. I found my car next to the rear *fourgon*, a black Swiss coach with red and white Maltese cross and placard on its side, reading "Paris-Berne via Dijon, Pontarlier, Neuchatel."

I boarded the second-class end of the carriage and looked for a smoking compartment. All were full. Even the aisle was crowded. I found a jump seat in the vestibule next to the door window, and there I settled down for the journey to Switzerland. I could hear outside the seemingly disorganized uproar of a French train departure; and yet, precisely on time, the shouting ceased and the train rolled out of the station, gathering speed along the banks of the Burgundy Canal, through the stucco suburbs and past the signal tower where a division occurred, one line going down the valley of the Rhone to Lyon, Marseilles, and the Riviera, the other branching off to Switzerland and Italy.

We followed this latter and were soon in open country, running fast over the plain that stretched eastward to the foothills and mountains of the Jura. I did not relish the four-hour journey on the hard seat, and to distract myself, I unfolded and read for the nth time a letter—a letter from a girl I had never met, and curiosity about whom was leading me to Neuchatel.

"Dear Jack," it read, "Your letter was wonderful. You must come. I need you. I haven't been able to find a place for you to stay. My French is hopeless and no one speaks my kind of German. Can't we leave your bag at the station and walk around till we find a room for you? It's not a huge town.

"I'm such a child it's ridiculous to react so vitally to unfavorable health and I think and hope I'm wrong that I have something simply awful the matter with me. What it can be to cause me to lie awake every night I really don't know. I hope you will.

"Please Jack, you will come, won't you? I can't abide one more weekend surrounded by chattering black uniformed French-Swiss jeunes filles. If you don't come soon I'll have to go home although I'm not expected until Christmas. The school doctor speaks and understands nothing but French and I with only English and German, really it's quite hopeless. Why did I ever come here? This is the most urgent plea of my life and funnily, it's not because you're my girl friend's boy friend's former roommate and someone from home I can talk to or a former med student who can possibly help me, but honestly because in a way it's you, the you of your letters. Am I hopelessly incoherent?

"I know you are terribly busy with your studies and all but it's awful to think there's a sane reason for your not coming. I wish you would let me wire you the money. I've never spent my allowance. I feel like a sick little cold little timorous yellow dog (did I hear you say bitch?). You will come Friday afternoon? I'll meet you at the *gare*. This is amusing, my crying out for help but so I am.

"Your needful, Nancy Clary."

I put the letter back in my pocket and mused over its contents, as the plain began to undulate into the first hills, and the bare trees be darkly interspersed with pines and firs. I would miss only the Friday laboratory. There was a *rapide* back on Sunday evening. I was curious about Nancy Clary, a student of the pipe organ, and said to be both beautiful and rich. And it was my first visit to Switzerland. It was called playing by ear. Would we make harmony or discord? I had no money to spare and would not take hers. It had been long since I had known an American girl. I was susceptible and yielded, and now the train was speeding toward a denouement. I dozed.

Pontarlier was the point of no return. From there most of the train went on to Geneva and through the Simplon Tunnel to Italy. My Swiss coach was coupled on to a waiting train drawn by an electric engine, and soon we were climbing through the last range of the Jura Mountains that separated France and Switzerland. Snow lay on the ground and clung to the branches of the firs. Crows flew up as the passing train disturbed them. Deep below in narrow pockets of the mountains were isolated villages, their houses plumed with chimney smoke. Here and there among the conifer forest, autumn-fired deciduous trees burned in shades of red and yellow. Then we crossed the frontier at Vallorbe, and soon were switchbacking down to the city on Lake Neuchatel.

I saw her on the platform as the train came to a stop: wind-blown blonde hair, expectant face, thin, worried and frowning, wrapped in a gray tweed coat. I went to her as she came along the platform.

"Thank God, you've come!" she said, as we shook hands in

continental fashion.

"Did you sleep better?"

"Not really. But I think it was excitement over your wire. Do you have more baggage?"

"Just this one. I'm not coming to stay. Let's find a place for me to sleep."

"I already did, just this morning. It's a *pension* room near here. I wish you would have let me pay for a hotel room."

"I can't afford to be in your power. A *pension* room is the limit of my budget."

"You'll let me take you to dinner."

"Where?"

"A perfect place on the lake front. I've already booked our table."

"Bart said you were bossy."

"He told me about you, too."

"I hope so."

"That you are a rebel."

"What else?"

"That you left a brilliant record at med school in San Francisco to bury yourself in a lab in the dreariest of provincial cities. Dijon must be frightfully ordinary."

"I suppose it would be for you. I am working and happy."

"Do you know any girls?"

"What kind of girls?"

"Girls you make love to."

"A different one each night."

"Bart said you were misanthropic."

"A love affair takes time. I've been busy."

"I warn you, I'm not going to have an affair with you."

"That's not why I came."

"Why then?"

"Because you asked me to."

"Do you always do what women ask you to?"

"When they are as blonde and beautiful as you are."

"Flattery will get you nowhere, Jack Burgoyne."

"I suppose it was really curiosity that brought me to Neuchatel."

"I have never known how you came by your last name."

"My paternal grandfather was French, named Bourgogne When he emigrated, he anglicized it. It means Burgundy."

"Is that why you chose Dijon?"

"Subconsciously, perhaps, but really for the endocrinology laboratory I'm working in. It has a wide reputation."

We chatted in pauses of climbing the steep street back of the station that led to the *pension*. At its door we turned and looked down on the terraced town, dropping to the lake. The sky was cloudy, the lake colorless, the Alps veiled.

"It's supposed to clear," she said, "and be milder. We're going on a picnic tomorrow."

"With the school?"

"Heavens, no! Just the two of us."

"Will I be safe?"

"Silly."

"Will you promise to stop frowning? You're getting a permanent wrinkle."

"It's worry. You must help me."

"I'm not a doctor."

"You'll let me tell you my symptoms?"

"For dessert."

"Don't tease me. I'm serious. I'll call for you at seven-thirty. You'll have time to change. I don't suppose you brought evening clothes."

"I don't have any."

"It *is* a chic restaurant."

"I have a dark suit on under my overcoat."

"I already tipped the headwaiter and told him we must have a quiet table where we can talk. May *I* dress?"

"In black."

"Bart said you were not to be trusted."

"A platonic affair will be a restful change."

"Don't count on anything more from me."

She went off down the steps and I settled in a large room with wash basin and wardrobe, and undressed for a nap. She posed a challenge. Was it really only for advice that she wanted me to come? The answer lay in pressing all the way.

Except for the frown and a brusque way of speaking, she was a lovely girl, although the heavy coat had concealed her figure.

A few minutes before seven-thirty I stood in front of the *pension* and waited for her. The sky had cleared. The stars glittered. Leaves from the plane trees rattled along the cobbled street. The air was sweet with woodsmoke. Below and in both directions were the lights of Neuchatel.

Then I heard a horse and carriage toiling up the street. It stopped and the driver swung down and opened the door for me. Nancy Clary was in the back seat. I got in and sat beside her. The driver wheeled, set his brake, and we went back down the hill, the horse's hooves ringing hesitantly on the cobbles, the brake shoes grinding on the iron-rimmed wheels.

"I have never ridden in a carriage," I said.

"I know you are going to help me. I just know you are."

She grasped my hand. I held hers. She withdrew it.

"I can't help it," I said. "You smell good. You and the woodsmoke."

"The townspeople lit fires in your honor. Do you like my perfume?"

"I thought it was you."

"Bart warned me."

"Can I help it if I'm responsive?"

"I've heard that before."

"So you know about men!"

"I'm no virgin, if that's what you are trying to find out."

"I wasn't, but I'm glad to know."

We reached the lake front and the horse began to trot along the avenue that followed the quay. We drew into a brilliantly lighted garden restaurant at the water's edge.

"Will you ask him to wait?" Nancy whispered to me.

"You mean through dinner?"

"Of course."

"I heard you were rich."

"I am—although the news from home is not good. Daddy says that the Depression is getting worse."

I did as she asked, and followed her into the restaurant. The headwaiter bowed and showed us to a corner table overlooking the lake; and as we gave up our coats and were seated, I saw Nancy's approving gaze.

"Did you expect me to be in corduroys?"

"Bart said you were unconventional."

"I wouldn't be here if I weren't."

"Thank you for dressing nicely. After all, we are a civilized people and should live that way."

"You talk like an old lady."

"I *am* twenty-five."

"And beautiful."

She was—in a low-cut, bare-armed, black evening gown, her hair done up and banded with a narrow black ribbon. Her eyes were blue, her lips a bit too thin.

"Do you like me?"

"If you'll stop frowning."

"But I'm worried."

"Stick out your tongue."

"I'm serious."

"I'm beginning to realize it. Can't we eat first? Pleasure before business. I'm starved."

"I'm sorry, Jack. I'll be patient."

"Be mine."

She wrinkled her nose at my pun.

Nancy had ordered the dinner, and it was a good one: filets of lake fish sautéed, with a local white wine, chilled and naturally sparkling, followed by *chateaubriand aux pommes frites* and watercress, and a bottle of Romanée.

"In your honor, Monsieur!" Nancy toasted, when the queen of the red Burgundies was served.

The food and drink made me expansive.

"Now, tell me your troubles, poor girl. Why can't Nancy sleep o'nights?"

"That's not it. That's not my real trouble, although I *might* just have a loathsome disease."

"You look disgustingly healthy, like a Swiss milkmaid."

"Horrible thought."

"Tell me."

"It's sex."

I laughed. *"That's* no trouble."

"Stop being so predatory."

"Men naturally are."

"Please listen to me." I went on eating and drinking while she talked. "I've known only two men. An English boy in Cheltenham and an Austrian man in Salzburg."

"As lovers?"

"Yes, but Jack," and she was almost in tears, "I never felt anything. Aren't I supposed to?"

"Normally."

"I've never—what do you call it what you have an orgasm?"

"Never come."

"I've tried so hard to. At first I blamed it on Roger, he was so young. Karl was a man though and very experienced."

She stopped, her eyes tearful.

"What happened?" I encouraged her.

"He cursed me. He said I was a blonde American bitch, as cold as the Arlberg Glacier."

I laughed.

"And you aren't?"

"It wasn't funny. I was never so humiliated. I loaned him money, too."

"And he never paid you back."

"How did you know?"

"I've read the classics."

"You keep making fun of me."

"After a meal like this? You're a marvelous cook."

"I hate to cook."

"Of course."

"What's wrong with me, Jack? Why can't I come? Don't all girls?"

"It's probably psychological."

"What do you mean?"

"You're too self-conscious."

"How do I go about forgetting myself?"

"It's late to start trying, if you haven't learned by now."

"Can you help me?"

"Do you want me to try?"

15

"No, if that's what you mean."
"You amuse me."
"I'm Irish, I warn you."
We listened to the string orchestra.
"Do you know what it is?" she asked.
"Yes."
"What?"
"Grieg's *Holberg Suite*."
"Bart never told me you were musical."
"I'm not. My mother was. She was a singer and a poet. I learned from her to love poetry and music. My father was a practical man."
"I came here for the course in pipe organ and found the Maître had gone on a tour. A young organist is in charge. I think he wants me to sleep with him."
"Well, why don't you?"
"I've suffered too much of a trauma."
"Didn't you ask me here to make love to you?"
"I did not."
"Why then?"
"For advice."
"You make it hard for me to help you. I might as well go back to Dijon."
"Not till Sunday, please."
"Will you stop frowning?"
"I'll try."
"You spoil your looks when you frown."
"Am I pretty?"
"Beautiful."
"Do I still smell sweet?"
"As all Burgundy."
"O Jack, I want so much to be normal."
"Let me hold your hand."
"Mother told me not to. She said the road to ruin began with holding hands."
"It's not a dirt road."
And so we held hands across the linen, and the meal ended harmoniously. As she was due in at eleven, I suggested that

16

the driver take her home first and then deliver me.

"Take this," she said, handing me a wad of francs. "Please pay for the meal and the carriage. Don't overtip, though; they don't expect it here in Neuchatel."

It was no place to argue. I took the money, paid the check and left a generous tip.

The driver had blanketed his horse, and he was great-coated; their breaths made frost on the air. The night was even sweeter with woodsmoke; and in the carriage, as we rolled smoothly along the lake front, Nancy's fragrance went to my head.

"You may leave your arm around me," she conceded.

"And kiss you?"

"Just one."

I was astonished when her mouth opened to mine and she relaxed in my arms.

We were at her school too soon.

"I said just one," she warned, as I sought to kiss her again.

"Tomorrow?"

"I've planned an outdoor day."

"I'm a great outdoorsman!"

"Meet me in the market place at nine-thirty," she said. "The driver will tell you where it is."

The concièrge opened the great front door and she slipped in and was gone. I paid the driver there, after getting directions to the market place, and found my way back up hill to my *pension* through drifts of wind-blown leaves. The night was cold, and I walked fast for warmth.

I was early for the rendezvous in the morning and wandered about the stalls. The foodstuffs were displayed with Swiss care and elegance—game, poultry, fruits and vegetables, breads and cheeses and sausages. The scene was bustling yet orderly, unlike the disorder of a French provincial market. The forecast proved true: it was a clear day of mild sunshine. The Alps were almost unreal, silhouetted against the pale sky.

Nancy found me in the throng. Again we shook hands.

"I slept!" she said.

"I lay awake."

"Thinking of me?"

"Thinking of it."

"You are a lecherous man."

"And you are a beautiful woman."

"Do you like me in this?"

She was wearing a tan skirt, a green flannel shirt, her hair in a loose knot at the back of her neck, green wool socks and ankle-high boots.

"Who wouldn't?"

"When you wrote that you wanted to walk in the autumn woods, I went shopping."

"I like women in skirts. They're more vulnerable."

"It's chamois—and so am I! You'll never catch me."

We packed her haversack with gruyère, ham, rye bread, and grapes. I slung it over my shoulder, and we set out for the *funiculaire* which took off from the highest terrace. A short steep ride brought us to the mountain top, high above city and lake, the woods at our back. A dirt track led deep into the colored fire of oak, chestnut, and ash; the last leaves of the year drifted around us like butterflies.

"This is my first real walk," she said. "We must not go too far. I'm not terribly strong."

"Is this the road to ruin your mother warned you of?"

"You'd better forget last night."

"That meal?"

"You know what I mean."

"Haven't you forgotten how to forget yourself?"

"I did, didn't I! But we really can't, here in Neuchatel. It's a very proper place."

"Aren't we beyond the city limits?"

"I'm not going to let you, so there."

"Well then, let's take it out in walking."

Toward noon we were passing a farmhouse, and I turned in and bought a litre wine-bottle of warm milk from a roomful of dung-booted peasants. They were gathered around a table in an open shed, husking a mountain of chestnuts.

We walked on out of sight, turned off the path, and while Nancy unpacked the food, I heaped up a drift of dry leaves. We devoured the nutty cheese, the smoky ham and coarse

18

bread, all washed down with milk, then savored the sugary grapes for dessert. I lay back on the leaves and looked up through bare boughs at the sky, while Nancy took a book from the haversack.

"Do you like German poetry?" she asked.

"Read me some and I'll decide."

"I bought this Insel Bücherei just for your coming. The poems are arranged by season."

"Is there a section called Indian Summer?"

"It is such a beautiful day."

"I didn't bring it with me. Dijon weather is horrible. It's fall, in case you aren't sure."

"Of the leaves, not me."

"You can't seem to get your mind off it. You'll end up giving *me* ideas."

"As long as you don't want to do more than talk."

"But I do!"

"I'm afraid of getting pregnant."

"You can trust me."

"Maybe someday. Could you come to Salzburg?"

"Paris would be the limit of my budget."

"I don't like the French."

"But I am American."

"A persistent one, too."

"Would you like it better if I were a woman?"

"I've never tried it with one."

"You're obviously made for man's enjoyment."

"But not yours, Jack Burgoyne. Please get that through your head."

"Well," I said, resignedly, "If we can't do it, let's read about it."

"I told you these are nature poems."

"Isn't it natural?"

"You're hopeless."

"I trust the situation isn't."

"I'll read you *Oktoberlied.*"

"It's November."

"Be quiet and listen."

19

She read beautifully. I stretched out in the crackling leaves, closed my eyes, and listened to her voice reading.

Der Nebel steigt, es fällt das Laub,
Schenk ein den Wein den holden;
Wir wollen uns den grauen Tag
Vergolden, ja vergolden.

"Translate, please."

"It means that in October there is rising mist and falling leaves and someone comes along and pours vintage wine, and the days are made golden; yes, golden."

"Yesterday was gray and windy and last night the world was all flying leaves. We drank wine and voilà; today is blue and gold." I caught her hand and sought to draw her down beside me. "O Nancy, your eyes are lake blue, sky blue, your hair is yellow gold, golden yellow."

She pulled loose. "Unhand me, varlet."

"Milk always makes me mellow."

She laughed. "You are an entertaining guest."

"Read me more, Miss Iceberg."

"Just don't call me a you know what."

"Don't be one and I won't."

She read Storm and Goethe, Rilke and Georg, and as I listened to her soft voice in the strange tongue, I heard only the music and not the meaning. I mused on what she would be like if she could forget herself. It did not seem hopeful. There was not time enough. And I was not patient.

I must have fallen asleep. When I opened my eyes, Nancy was asleep beside me, no trace of frown on her thin face, her breathing deep and regular. I leaned over her on my elbow. She opened her eyes and frowned. The spell was broken. I stood up.

"En route, mademoiselle," I said, helping her up.

We walked slowly back out of the woods and again looked down on the terraced town and lake and across to the Alps, rosy in the afternoon light. We saw a dirt road leading to terrace after terrace, and instead of taking the *funiculaire*, we decided to walk all the way down. We heard the sounds of children at play, of barking dogs, tramcars, and church bells striking the hour. Peasant women were gleaning in the vineyards. We leaned on a stone wall and rested, while a gleaner crept toward us along the row. When she reached the end at the wall, she straightened to turn and go back, saw us and croaked, "Bon soir, m'sieu, 'dame. Vous vous promenez? Qu'il fait beau aujourd'hui! Mais dépêchons-nous, il va pleuvoir." She waved toward the Alps and the gathering clouds, then resumed her gleaning.

"I'm so glad we came this way," Nancy said, squeezing my hand.

We kept descending toward the town. The air was perfumed with smoke from burning leaves, rising from many points in town. Nancy began to limp from a tight boot, and as we neared my *pension*, I suggested we stop there and rest. I expected her to say no. Instead she agreed. At an *épicerie* I bought a kilo of Algerian dates and a bottle of vin rosé.

"I shouldn't have come," she said, as I closed my room's door and locked it. "But I am so tired."

"Lie down, and let me take off your boots."

She was passive as I unlaced and removed them and then her heavy socks. Her legs were smooth and white. She wiggled her toes in relief. I wet a washcloth.

"That's heavenly," she murmured, as I bathed her feet.

"Your role's reversed, Mary Magdalen."

"I never walked so far in all my life."

"Drink this." I poured her a glass of wine, and I, too, drank a full glass. We ate dates. I sat on the edge of the bed. Her eyes were closed. I began to caress her forehead and to stroke her hair and neck. Her arms reached up and drew me down, and our mouths met again in a wet and winy kiss.

She finally broke away. I said nothing.

"My skirt will be ruined," she murmured, arching her back. "Be a good Jack."

I pulled it off and threw it on a chair.

"Hang it up, please," she whispered.

"To hell with it," I said, fearing to break the spell. I found her mouth again and she returned my kiss, even more passionately. My hand slid down to remove her panties and again she arched her back.

There came a stern rapping on the door.

"Who is it?" I called.

"The landlady. You have left mud on the hall rug. Kindly remove your soiled shoes hereafter when you enter."

"As you desire, Madame, I shall not give offense another time."

I had gotten up to go to the door, and now turned back to the bed, groaning, "Ah God, the tidy Swiss!" Nancy was sitting up.

"Give me my skirt. I've changed my mind."

I pushed her down. "Change it back."

"I won't."

"I'm going to make love to you, if it's the last thing I do."

"It will be the last thing if you do. Let me up."

I held her down. She struggled silently. I pinned her against the wall.

"Come on, Jack," she said, matter of fact, "you can't make me."

"You've heard of rape."

"What pleasure would that give you?"

"Lots."

"You're an egotistical bastard, Jack Burgoyne, and I hate you. I'll *never* let you now. Please give me my skirt."

I threw it high on the wardrobe.

"Don't do that! It's an expensive skirt. You'll ruin it."

"I'll ruin you."

"You've ruined it all, just as I was giving in."

"Give in again."

"Jack, listen to me, I must get back and change, and there's the concert at 8:30. I bought box seats for us."

"We'll make our own music."

"You tried to get me drunk and you almost did." She turned face down, sobbing.

Time passed. I sat on the edge of the bed and would not let her up in spite of her alternate pleading and scolding. I drank the rest of the wine. I was a little drunk, and disgusted by the

22

way things had miscarried.

At last I relented. I stood on a chair and threw her the chamois skirt. She slipped into it, unlocked the door and was gone. I looked at my watch. It was ten o'clock. I went to the window and threw it open. The street and walks were glistening. The wind had risen and rain was blowing.

I started to undress, and then I relented, hurried into my clothes, took my overcoat, and went out. She was sheltering under a nearby fir tree. I threw my coat around her and we hurried silently back to her school. I was cold sober, ashamed of having overplayed my hand. While waiting for the concièrge to open, she removed my coat and I put it on over my wet clothes.

"Thank you at last for being a gentleman," she said, coldly.

"At your service, Miss Blondebitch." I bowed and walked away, as the door closed. I trudged back to my room through the empty streets. The leaves underfoot were sodden.

I was awakened in the morning by a soft knocking on the door.

"Who is there?" I called, expecting the landlady to answer.

"It's me, Nancy. Let me in."

I got up and unlocked the door. She pushed by me.

"How did you sleep, Mr. Caveman?"

I did not answer, and began to wash my face and comb my hair.

"I slept," she offered.

"I didn't expect to see you again."

"I came for my haversack."

"It's there in the corner."

"Don't be cross with me, Jack. Kiss me good morning. Or do you insist on shaving first?"

"I'm taking the noon train."

"It's an *express* and it stops everywhere. Please take the 20:30 *rapide*."

"What would I do with myself until then?"

"Be with me."

"What do you mean?"

"What I say."

"We behaved badly."

23

"I'll take the blame, if you'll stay. Please stay. I need you. I've felt so well since you came." She took my hand. "I lost my head when she knocked. Forgive me." She embraced me. I breathed her freshness of hair and skin and soap. "We can go back to our bed of leaves."

"It rained."

"We can stay here."

"What if she knocked again?"

"Keep our heads under the covers."

"This is a new Nancy."

"Don't be cross with me. Nancy loves Jack. Nancy will offer proof of her love if Jack wishes."

"Carnal?"

"Utterly."

"Nancy Clary in the role of Delilah. Instead of cutting my hair, will you shave me?"

"Put on the lather."

We laughed. "Wait for me out front," I said. "I'll shave and dress and be right down."

"Will we come back here?"

"All I can think of now is my stomach. We'll take care of the other organs later."

"I have never known anyone as outspoken as you."

"I can't help it."

"I'm accustomed to more genteel persons, but I'm beginning to like you, Jack Burgoyne."

"I'm willing to start over. Are you going to wait outside for me?"

"No, I want to watch you shave."

"Where will we eat?"

"I know a nice place on the lake front where we can have petit déjeuner."

"I want breakfast, lunch, and dinner. Dates is all I've had since yesterday noon."

"Poor man, Nancy will feed you."

I felt my interest rising as she showed this contrite side of her nature. The day was fair after rain, and it was an attractive outdoor restaurant on the quay, under pollarded plane trees, the water of the lake all but lapping our table as we ordered a mushroom omelette and ham, bread and sweet butter and jam, with café au lait. Under the morning sun the lake was dancing with whitecaps. Fresh snow had whitened the Alps. The promenade was peopled with the Neuchatelois in their Sunday best. They were a staid folk all dressed in black.

While I ate hungrily Nancy nibbled at her plate; and she, too, was silent until finally she looked at her wrist watch and said,

"You've missed the noon train. I was afraid you might change your mind. Now you're mine until tonight."

"Possessive, aren't you? I must say, though, I like the new Nancy."

"You've done it. I hate myself for panicking. I knew it would have happened."

"What would have?"

"Do I have to say it?"

"Yes."

"I felt myself having an . . . I felt myself . . . coming."

"What was it like?"

"Fire under the ice. I felt myself beginning to melt and flow."

"There's hope for you. You haven't frowned once this morning."

"You don't hate me?"

"You're too selfish."

"So are you. You came just to have a good time at my expense."

"To have a good time together. That way we cancel each other's selfishness."

"I ruined it."

"You'll do it again if you keep talking about it."

"I want more than anything to be normal—and not pregnant."

"No danger with your Uncle John."

"Do you know why I am not frowning? Because I know that something nice is going to happen to me."

"You *can* be sweet, Nancy Clary."

"And we will turn the gloomy days to golden days, yes, golden."

25

"Did you bring the little book?"

"Only my fair young body and my long golden hair."

It went the way she wanted and that I had hoped, the day before, it would go. We returned to my room, undressed, and lay on the bed. She was beautiful and good to love, with no trouble between us and no knock on the door. Somewhere in the *pension* a violinist was practicing Bach sonatas; and as we lay quietly afterward, Nancy hummed along with him. Sunday in Neuchatel was dead quiet. No noise rose from the street. We slept and then made love again.

When it grew dark, we dressed; I packed my bag, and we walked to the station for supper in the buffet.

"I'm starved again," I confessed.

"The stomach is terribly important in your scheme of things."

"I have a rapid rate of metabolism."

"I'm so glad I'm normal. It was so good. For the first time in my life. But I wonder?" She clung to my arm, and I saw that she was frowning.

"Now what's the matter?"

"Jack, are you sure I'm all right?"

"You mean pregnant?"

"Silly! I mean *not* pregnant."

"Of course you won't be. Didn't I explain to you?"

"I know, but what if there was a leak?"

"Should I have blown them up?"

"Don't be sarcastic."

"Then don't worry."

"Women are born to worry."

"Give me one that doesn't and I'll make her my goddess."

"You're not the one who will swell up and be horrid looking."

We had reached the station, taken a table in the buffet, and ordered dinner of roast lamb and white beans and a chicory salad. Nancy would not eat. Her hair began to come down and she went to the rest room to pin it up. When she returned, she was frowning.

"I know you think I'm impossible," she said, "but I really think I'd better go home and take a douche."

26

"Eat something first. See me off, then take a carriage. You'll be all right. Let me pour you some wine."

"I know you think I'm always spoiling it for you."

"You are."

"And I'm frowning horribly."

"You're not pretty anymore."

"I don't care. I just can't eat. She smiled wanly. "I think I have evening sickness. Please get me a carriage."

"Do you mean it?"

"Please, I must go."

I followed her outside to the carriage rank.

"Get in with me, Jack, and sit a minute. Kiss me good-by."

"You have a genius for ruining things."

"Wasn't it worth it?"

"A thousand times no," I said cruelly.

"Won't you kiss me good-bye?"

"No."

"Will you take this money?"

"No."

"You are heartless."

"Only when you make me so."

"Please, Jack." She began to cry.

I turned away and went toward the buffet door. I heard the carriage door close, the wheels grinding on the cobbles as it turned, and the horse's hooves beginning the deliberate klop klop, as it drove away.

Though full of self-disgust, I ate both portions of the lamb and beans and salad and was on the platform as the *rapide* from Berne came in, silently drawn by an electric engine. This time I found an empty compartment in the through car to Dijon and Paris, stretched out on the wide seat with my overcoat for a blanket, and soon fell asleep to the clicking of wheels over the rail points.

II

Erda

What draws a man to a woman—that draws one man to one woman when they are only two among thousands? In the beginning it was probably because she went bareheaded even in the coldest weather. Her hair was the color of ripening cornsilk. It hung to her shoulders in rippling waves and gleamed in the winter sunlight. She was short and solidly built, with a strong stride. Each noonday when she passed the café window as I was taking an apéritif, I watched her come up the Rue Chabot-Charny, probably from the Faculty of Letters, cross the Place du Théâtre to the sidewalk outside the window where I sat, then on past the Church of St. Michel and out of sight.

She was obviously not French. High cheekbones and aquiline nose indicated what race? Slav? Magyar? Finn? I came to await her daily passage, a kind of princess among the provincial throng that streamed by each day on the way home to lunch; and though I stared at her coming, her passing profile, and her going, never did she notice me.

After she had gone, I mused over my vin blanc-cassis. Should I follow her and learn where she lived? Or block her way and introduce myself? I did neither. I was wary of all blondes after Neuchatel; and yet, though I was occupied in laboratory work, with little free time, I wanted the company of a woman. No Dijonnaise drew me. The sweetness I had tasted with Nancy, although it had turned bitter, was like honey at the back of my tongue.

Then one afternoon, because I was interested in the Symbolists, I went to a five o'clock lecture, given by the Dean at the Faculty of Letters, on Rimbaud, the wonder boy of French poetry. She was there. I saw her a few rows below me in the petit-amphithéâtre. Throughout the Dean's crisp, logical, and elegant *explication*, I stared down at her, seated to one side so that I could watch her face partly in profile, strong yet not masculine, wide, generous mouth, large forehead. She seemed spellbound, never turning her gaze from the short, dark, fox-like speaker. The hour went by. My mind was divided, following the Dean's lecture and at the same time dreaming of her who fascinated me, wondering how to draw her to me as I was drawn to her.

"Lucid, yet mystical," the Dean concluded, "as in these lines, saying all, meaning what? Take them with you, listeners, as a talisman in memory." He lowered his voice, and read:

> *J'ai fait la magique étude*
> *Du bonheur, que nul n'élude.*
> *O vive lui, chaque fois*
> *Que chante le coq gaulois.*

The applause was loud and long. The Dean acknowledged it with a sardonic smile. The students waited for him to leave the platform, then they crowded into the aisles. I stood at the back, watching her come up the steps; and then as she approached, drawing on her gloves, I took a deep breath, stepped in her way, and heard myself say,

"Je demande pardon, mademoiselle, mais puis-je vous accompagner chez vous?"

Her blue eyes stared into mine, and for a second I feared defeat. Then she smiled and said in English,

"If you like."

"But . . . but . . ." I stammered, "you are not English."

"I prefer it to French."

"You speak it beautifully."

"How nice of you to say that."

"English English, not American English."

"Will you teach me American English?"

"How did you know I am American?"

"I am a wise woman."

"What are you?"

"Do you wish to see my papers?"

"Forgive my curiosity."

"Guess."

"Finnish? Esthonian?"

"You speak like a world traveller."

"Hungarian? Russian?"

She shook her head.

"I give up. I only know that you are the most beautiful woman in Dijon."

She laughed delightedly. "I'm an ordinary Swede from Stockholm."

"I am an extraordinary American."

She laughed. "From San Diego."

"How did you know?"

"The nephew of the lady who keeps the *pension* is a colleague of yours at the Faculty."

"Who?"

"Raoul Dupont. He has told me of you, the lone American, the recluse, the woman hater, so regular in his habits, so intelligent and brilliant—a genius *enfin*."

"I thought the Swedes were serious, but you are a tease. What is your name?"

"Erda."

"Erda what?"

"Erda Lindström."

"Erda means earth. What does Lindström mean?"

"It means linden stream."

"I'm John Burgoyne."

"May I call you Johnny?"

Throughout the conversation we were partly blocking the aisle, oblivious of the push and jostle of the students; and it was she who finally took my arm and steered us out onto the street.

It was dark, the street thick with bicyclists, furiously ringing their bells as they rode home from work, candled lanterns swinging from their handlebars. We walked along the sidewalk toward the Place du Théâtre, and when it narrowed, I dropped off into the cobbled gutter. As we crossed the Place and approached the café, she squeezed my arm and said, "That's where you sit at noon."

"You've seen me?"

"Like a fish in an aquarium."

"And I thought I was studying you."

"Don't you know how perceptive women are?"

"Sometimes I forget. An apéritif now?"

"I am not supposed to, unchaperoned. Yet I will with you."

We entered the warm, smoky café and sat side by side on the leather *banc* against the wall, under an ornate gilt-framed mirror, with another across from us in which we could see ourselves. The room was rumbling with Burgundian French, over which her English accent sounded exquisite.

"You like poetry," I said.

"Not particularly."

"Why were you there?"

"Madame Décat says that the Dean speaks the purest French in Dijon. He bored me, so logical, like a scientist dissecting a butterfly."

"He looks like a fox that's raided the hencoop."

"She says he has a very bad character."

"Did you see me?"

"I felt you."

"You knew I was there?"

"Why didn't you come sit with me? I thought Americans were friendly."

"My grandfather was French."

"The French aren't shy."

"I'm not very typical anything, I guess. Are you enrolled in Letters?"

"I go for the learning, not for a diploma."

"What are you doing in Dijon?"

"It's called *absorbing culture*. I was in Germany, Italy, England."

"Where next?"

"Home."

"When?'

"In three more weeks."

"May I see you again?''

"Madame Décat has not encouraged me to have rendezvous."

"She's not running a convent, is she?"

"Madame is strict. Raoul will vouch for you though. In fact, he already has."

"You know more about me than I do about you."

"It is a woman's way."

"How old are you?"

"Guess."

"Twenty-four."

"I am only eighteen."

"You are so womanly."

"We women of the north mature early."

"I have been led to believe that Swedes are a somber people."

"Laplanders and Norwegians, perhaps; Swedes and Danes—toujours gai!"

"You have had men friends here?"

"The Dijonnais do not interest me."

"What do you like to do?"

"Ski. The Côte-d'Or is no place for ski-ing."

"Do you like to walk?"

"Very much. I am strong."

"Music?"

"Oh, yes!"

"Would Madame allow you to go to the opera with me a week from Saturday?"

"Come home with me and ask her."

"And for a walk this Sunday?"

"I'll say yes to all that you ask of me."

Such was our beginning. Erda was extroverted, unsentimental, vigorous, and healthy. We shook hands in meeting and parting, and her grip was as strong as mine. In the beginning we were like brother and sister. She resembled an American college girl in her forthright manner, but with flashes of an exotic foreign cast of mind. I called her my blonde Viking. She did not show any romantic interest in me or in anything.

Our night at the opera changed that. It was a one-night stand by a company from Paris. Dijon's shabby municipal theater across from the café was packed with the town's élite. Erda was beautiful in a sea-green gown which revealed her strong white arms, shoulders, and neck. Her hair was done up in a severe coiffure. She was eye-catching amidst the over-dressed, heavily perfumed throng, and I saw several of my professors stare at her, then wink knowingly at me. I was enormously pleased with myself.

The opera was Moussorgsky's *Boris*, its music passionate enough to overcome such handicaps as rickety scenery, dusty stage, ragged orchestra, an off-key soprano and a restless audience used to Puccini and Massenet. The bass who sang Boris, however, was superb, and the bells of the Kremlin, rung off-stage, were deafening. At the climax of Boris's death, I saw tears on Erda's cheek. Her hand reached mine and squeezed it hard.

As we walked home from the theater, she clung to my arm and was quieter than I had ever known her. It was a clear night, the stars like bright powder, and our breaths made frost on the air.

"You were moved by it," I said.

"Oh Johnny, I never knew music could be like that."

"Hearing it together does it."

"With you, Johnny, with you."

She was transformed from the tomboy I had known before. All my senses were heightened by the knowledge. As we neared the Rue de Metz, our heels ringing on the cobbles, we saw a glow ahead and hurried toward it. A building was on fire. The occupants had fled to the street in night clothes and coats. A crowd stood transfixed, their faces raised like flowers to the fiery spectacle. Firemen were coupling hoses and raising ladders and commanding the people to stand back. No one moved. Blue flames spurted from the metal gutters. Window glass cracked and crashed. The roof suddenly burned through and a fountain of sparks played into the windless sky. The crowd gasped.

We shoved into the thick of it, Erda clinging to my side, and there we stood pressed together, surrounded by people oblivious of each other. Erda began to tremble.

"Cold?" I whispered, drawing her closer.

She did not answer.

I felt my way beneath her fur coat. Her body was hot. She

pressed even closer and whispered in my ear,

"I hope they never get it out."

My own excitement mounted as I realized that the fire had aroused her. I moved so that I stood in back of her and let my hands, still beneath her coat, begin to caress her breasts and belly. No one paid the least attention to us, their faces ruddy in the glow. My lips found her warm neck. My hands grew more ardent. Her breath quickened and suddenly her body went rigid. My arms tightened around her until she slowly relaxed and would have slumped to the ground had I not held her fast.

"We must go," she whispered finally. "I promised Madame I would come home after the opera."

We forced our way out of the crowd and hurried the rest of the way to her *pension*. As she searched in her bag for the door key, I sought to kiss her. To my astonishment she broke free, slapped me hard, and cried, "Let me go." She opened the door and it slammed in my face.

I stood for a moment, then walked home through the empty streets. The wind had risen and window shutters were banging in the still of the night.

A week passed. My puzzlement changed to anger at the way she had reacted. I moved across the Place to the Café de la Comédie for my noontime drink and did not see her pass. Then on the following Saturday morning Raoul Dupont brought a note from Erda, asking me to have Sunday lunch at her *pension* and go for a walk afterward. I told him to tell her yes. I wanted badly to see her again.

Madame Décat was well known in Dijon for her culture. Before she had been widowed by the war, her home was a salon. Now it was an exclusive *pension* for foreign girls. She was petite with gray hair and pale blue eyes and a lovely sad face. Luncheon was formal. Erda and I were elaborately polite to one another. I had no eyes for the other girls, but directed my attention to the hostess. Raoul was in Paris, and except for the butler I was the only man present. Madame Décat led the talk through topics as varied as the comparative sweetness of Spanish and Californian oranges, the preparation of Burgundian snails for cooking, the amount of honey in the best Dijon gingerbread, the limestone formations of the Côte-d'Or, the music of Rameau and the sermons of Bossuet, two of Dijon's most glorious native sons. The talk was lively. She knew something about everything. The food was elegant, and in my honor she opened a vintage bottle of Clos Vougeot, a heady red Burgundy.

After lunch, and the girls had dispersed and Erda was changing into walking clothes, I found myself alone in the parlor with Madame Décat.

"Let me get to the point," she said softly. "You are aware, I am sure, Monsieur Burgoyne, that Mademoiselle Lindström's parents have charged me with responsibility for their daughter while she is under my roof."

"I assumed she must have parents," I countered, "although she has never referred to them."

"Although she obviously possesses some of the attributes of a woman, she is still a girl, and of fluctuating emotions. Since you escorted her to the opera, she has been in a rather high state of nerves."

"Music affects some in this way."

She smiled faintly, then said, "As a student of human nature, as well as of the more exact sciences, you are familiar with the psychology of infatuation."

"I assure you, Madame, of the honor of my intentions. Erda will testify to the platonic nature of our relationship. To speak the truth, I have not seen her since that evening."

"Just so. I know something of your lineage, Monsieur Burgoyne, or you would not be my guest today. But I must inform you, inasmuch as she tells me that she has not done so, that Mademoiselle Lindström is affianced."

"To whom?"

"To one of Stockholm's most substantial financiers. A banker, to be precise, and a widower of an age, it is true, considerably more advanced than hers. A most distinguished individual, I am told, and of great means. She is spending these months abroad at his instance, chaperoned, to be sure, in order that she may prepare herself to be the lady of his house."

"We do not favor such marriages in our land."

"Customs vary, as we observed in our conversation at the luncheon table. One learns tolerance."

"I am not planning an elopement," I protested.

Madame Décat arched her thin brows and shrugged her shoulders. "I am convinced of the truth of all you say. But here is the point my dear young man, here is the point I have taken far too long to arrive at—and I beg of you to forgive my prolixity—I should not care to see your relationship with her transformed into something more ardent. Mademoiselle is young, I repeat, and though fully developed as a woman in body—indeed most seductively so, I am fully prepared to admit—and accomplished beyond the average in such diverse interests as sports and languages, the creature is still essentially a naïve."

"This is indeed part of her charm."

Madame Décat again ventured a small sad smile. "Raoul was right. You are truly not a crude foreigner; so unlike the Americans we are accustomed to, thick tongued and heavy handed. Your perceptions and reactions are altogether Gallic."

"My grandfather was French," I reminded her. "From Auxerre."

"The purest of Burgundian. And you, my esteemed friend, are a very likeable young man."

"Thank you, Madame. What is your price for this fine compliment?"

She chuckled. "Raoul did not sufficiently emphasize your roguishness." Her face hardened. "I will tell you. It is imperative that Mademoiselle Lindström leave Dijon in the same state in which she arrived in my care."

"And that is precisely what?"

"A virgin, my dear son, a virgin."

"But my dear Madame, we have been as brother and sister. We have never exchanged—I hesitate to say enjoyed—a single kiss."

Again she gave me a tired, wise, and compassionate smile, then flared her eyes and said, "This is her last week in Dijon;" and added with icy precision, "I am counting on your honor as an erstwhile neophyte of Hippocrates to see that she leaves Dijon—and may I borrow a phrase from your discipline—that she leaves Dijon *virga intacta.*"

Erda entered the parlor at that moment and I made no reply. I thanked my hostess for a delicious lunch, bowed and kissed her hand, and Erda and I took our leave

As we walked through the curving narrow streets and reached the aspe of Notre Dame, Erda halted and drew off her glove.

"You must also remove yours," she said, and when I had done so, she took my hand and placed it on a little owl carved in relief on the stone of the church.

"What is it?" I asked.

"The wishing owl. See how smooth it is worn?" She put her hand over mine. "Now wish together." And after a pause, "Have you wished?"

"Yes. Shall I tell you what?"

"Then it wouldn't come true."

"Tell me yours."

"Guess."

"The same as mine?"

"Yes."

The afternoon was bitter cold and we walked fast to keep warm, stride for stride, her arm in mine, neither speaking, until we reached the park on the edge of town. It was about a mile square and been created in the seventeenth century by Le Notre, the great landscape architect. The incidental details of his original design had long since vanished, and there remained only the basic geometrical pattern of unpaved walks and intermediate groves of ancient trees, now stripped bare to a company of skeletons. The park's southern limit was the little Ouche River, and there on a stone bench at its edge we rested. Although barely four o'clock, the sun was low in the sky and there was no warmth from its rays. We gathered leaves and twigs and lit a fire, took off our gloves and warmed our hands. Crows rose from the stubble field across the semifrozen river and cawed their heavy way toward the low sun. The time was winter and everything was numbed and slow. The sweet smoke from the fire rose without wavering.

"Why have you avoided me?" she finally broke the silence. "Was it because I slapped you?"

"Partly."

"Is there someone else?"

"No."

"I was frightened by my feelings. I have always been sure of myself."

"You were so responsive."

"It was the music and the fire—and your hands and lips."

"I didn't want to let you go."

"All week I have longed for you."

"We are together now."

"Madame Décat would surely reprove me for my boldness, but I must say it. Do you want to hear it?"

"Tell me."

"I love you."

We stood up and I took her in my arms and sought to kiss her.

"No," she said. "You must tell me first what you and she were talking about."

"More about snails and oranges."

"Liar. I saw her face."

"She told me what is going to happen when you go home."

"Oh, I hate her for that! Johnny, I swear I don't love him."

"But you are going to marry him."

"Yes, I am."

"You foreigners have quaint ways."

"Don't be sarcastic. I am going away in another week. Have you thought of me at all?"

"Every night."

"Oh Johnny, kiss me now."

Our first kiss was long and deep and tender, while her gloved hands stroked my face. She was radiant as my hands found her again under her coat.

"I am so happy," she said. "Can we walk again before I leave?"

"Lab keeps me until five every day and by then it is pitch

dark. Can you come at noon?"

"Madame made me promise not to, even with you."

"Evening?"

"I am all but locked in my room."

"She is a veritable watchdog. A pity she has forgotten her youth."

"She has never forgiven life for having left her a widow."

I looked at my watch. "If we hurry, we can hear a concert from Paris."

"What do you mean?"

"Sundays before you came, I always went to a friend's house for the five o'clock radio-diffused concert from the Conservatoire. It won't be like the other night, but I think you'd enjoy it."

My friend was an old French *confiseur* from the Vosges who had retired to a family property in Dijon, a great eighteenth century *hotel* in the Rue Berbisey, where he spent hours huddled over the loud-speaker, tuning in music from all over Europe. He lived alone and welcomed my weekly visit while we sat silently in the formal parlor, listening to the broadcast and nibbling a plate of his sweets, with a liqueur.

We found Monsieur Bonespoir fighting static, as he struggled to bring in the Paris broadcast.

"You honor me to return," he greeted us, "and to bring with you such a charming creature. I must apologize for the cold. I suggest you leave on your coats."

The pink-eyed, walrus-mustached, portly old candymaker had on his coat, hat, muffler, and gloves, while he muttered and twirled the dials and cursed the crackling interference. Then all of a sudden Radio Paris came in bell-clear and the concert commenced with the *Roman Carnival* overture.

"Enfin!" he beamed and brought out a plate of cookies and gingerbread and poured us tiny glasses of kümmel, where Erda and I sat at a great square table, covered with green baize and over which hung a beaded chandelier with one bulb of low wattage.

The Berlioz was followed by a song-cycle for soprano and orchestra, a *première audition* of *Les Heures du Foyer*, a suite

41

of lullabies sung by an expectant mother, seated at the fireside, to her unborn child. It was followed by the *Daphnis and Chloe* music, an orgy of sound that made Erda's eyes shine and her hand reach for mine.

Old Bonespoir joined us at the table during the entr'acte.

"You also like music?" he asked her.

"Oh yes!"

"You must come again with Monsieur Jean."

"Alas, I leave in another week."

"Where do you go?"

"My home is in Stockholm."

"Tiens," he exclaimed, "the other side of the moon."

"You have travelled?"

"Once to Grasse, for a particular perfumed condiment."

The final music was the César Franck symphony. We were carried away on the flood of sonority, holding hands, staring at one another across the table in the dim light.

The concert ended and the old man saw us to the door.

"Did I ever tell you?" he asked me, "that Sophie and Mirabeau occupied these chambers on their elopement from Paris? Your coming here, so close do you seem one to the other, reminded me of those passionate ones." He shook our hands and murmured, "Ah, la belle jeunesse!"

The door closed. We crossed the flagstone courtyard in the biting air and the great wooden street door slammed on our backs like doom. We hurried through the narrow streets that formed the mazy heart of the old town, for it was after seven and she was late. We stood a moment at the door of her *pension*, but when I sought again to reach beneath her coat, she pushed me away.

"I dare not. We must say farewell. Adieu, my love." She kissed my cheek and was gone. I walked away down the curving street, my desire not cooled by the snow that had begun to drift down in the dark.

The days passed. I kept vigil at the café. In vain. Perhaps she had left before the appointed time. Then I learned from Raoul that Erda was still in Dijon and was leaving on Friday. On Thursday all of the faculties of the university were closed, along with other state institutions, because of the funeral in Paris of a war hero. The day was cold and rainy, and I remained in my room. As the bell clock on the municipal library tolled three, there was a knock on my door.

"Come in," I called, seated at my work table, my back to the door, believing it to be the chambermaid with clean towels.

The door opened and a moment later from in back of my chair cold soap-sweet hands closed over my eyes.

"Guess who!"

"Erda!"

I stood up and took her in my arms. Her cheeks were cold, her lips warm.

"I have longed to see you," I said.

"You sent no word."

"I waited each noon."

"I took another route, pausing each day at the wishing owl."

"I went there one day and wished. And now do we not have our wish?"

"I was afraid. I have promised Madame Décat that it would be our last rendezvous. I hoped that somehow you would find me and then I would not break my promise."

"I despaired, particularly when you parted so casually."

"Oh Johnny, you must not say that! I am not casual. I am a frightened girl. I have never known these feelings."

"I thought you northern women matured early."

"I was teasing you. I will not tease you any longer. When Raoul reported the faculty closed today, I had an overpowering desire to be with you. Promise or no, I came."

"In the wind and the rain. Take off your coat and let me hang it to dry."

"I brought you a present for your little phonograph." She took a parcel from the bed. I opened it and found a recording of Franck's *Variations Symphoniques*. I put it on. Erda looked around my room at books and pictures. She found a bottle of Sandeman's ruby port and poured us each a glass.

"Skaal!" she toasted, and sat cross-legged on the floor beside my chair.

I removed her wet beret and her hair fell loosely to her shoulders, silky and fragrant. I whispered in her ear, "Look up. Let me see your face. You are thinner. There are circles under your eyes."

"I have thought of you in the sleepless night. Yesterday while shopping with Madame, I heard this record and I returned today and bought it for you. I wanted us to hear it together."

"My darling."

"I brought you something else."

"What?"

"You might not want it now. How can I say it?"

"Whisper in my ear."

I slipped to the floor beside her and for a moment we were joined in a kiss. Then she freed herself and said,

"It is myself that I bring you." And then, even softer and in French, "Parceque je vous aime. Je vous . . . je t'aime, tu sais."

Again we kissed, but I could not forget our predicament. It was a student *pension*. There were no locks on the doors. People came and went in great informality. The nosy chambermaid was everywhere at all hours.

I lifted Erda up and we went to the window. I opened it and we looked down on the rainy street and across to the wine merchant's courtyard where workmen were rolling barrels across the cobbles to the cellar chute. The lamplighter was making his rounds in the darkening afternoon and stopped beneath us to raise his long, lighted taper and thrust it up into the bracketed lamp which in a moment began to glow with golden light.

"Do that to me," she said, seeking my lips, "Oh Johnny, do that to me."

"We must cool off," I said. "There is no privacy, and besides, we deserve at least a night, not an hour."

"But how? The Décat has become so vigilant. I leave tomorrow. She knows that I love you. I told her so. I want to tell everyone. I wanted to call down to the lamplighter."

The rain blew in on us as we stood together and kissed.

There came a knock on the door and even before I could call "Entrez!" the chambermaid burst in with the towels.

"Pardon," she said, "I was unaware that Monsieur had company." She gave me a knowing look, arranged the towels with elaborate care, and finally went out.

"See what I mean?"

"Play the record again. Music fertilizes my brain."

We stood at the window in a close embrace all through the *Variations*, and then she spoke.

"Would you love me in Paris?"

"What are you saying?"

"Could you join me there?"

"But how? You are going home to be married."

"To a man I love not. That old Croesus shall not have me first."

"But how?"

"I am not supposed to tarry in Paris, of course. Madame is putting me on the train tomorrow and I am to taxi from Gare de Lyon to Gare du Nord and take the Nord Express to Hamburg where my fiancé's agent is to meet me."

"You are booked through to Stockholm?"

"Stopovers are permitted."

"With whom?"

"I have excellent friends there whom my family would trust to chaperone me. A young Swedish married couple studying at the Beaux-Arts."

"Would they delegate the chaperonage to me?"

"I stopped over with them on my way here in October and they were sympathetic to my plight. They would gladly aid me in a deception of Old Moneybags. They would join me in a telegram to my parents, and then you and I could be together for a few days, even for a week, if you did not tire of me."

"A week of nights."

"As you desire. Can you leave your work?"

"I can make it up."

"I have enough money left for us both."

"I have some," I lied, knowing that I would have to borrow. "When does your train leave?"

"The two-thirty *rapide* from Lyon."

"What class?"

"First. You must board without her seeing you. She's hardly worried now though. She believes her little lecture cooled you off. I, too, feared that it had."

"Raoul won't give us away?"

"Tell him you've been called to Switzerland again."

"Of course. On banking business."

"Oh Johnny, I want you to have me first!"

"And I want you. Wait and see."

We pledged the rendezvous with a kiss and she left. I leaned out the window and saw her wave as she hurried up the Rue de Petit-Potet.

I went early to the station the next day, taking a back way along the canal path, carrying a suitcase and wearing my overcoat, for the cold had settled down for the winter and the sun was seen no more. I checked my bag to Paris, then gained the platform and walked along in the direction of Lyon out into the freight yards, and there I waited for the *rapide* to arrive, certain that I was out of sight even if Madame Décat should accompany Erda to the platform.

Once again I was going to a romantic rendezvous, but this time in place of the curiosity that was a main part of my motivation in meeting Nancy in Switzerland, I felt mounting desire to be with Erda in Paris and to satisfy the passion I knew she was capable of. Compounding the intensity of my feeling was the excitement of eluding Madame Décat's vigilance and of cheating the old Swedish banker of his interest due.

I heard the *rapide's* shriek as it entered the yards and then saw the huge engine bearing down on me and the long train roll past and come to a stop a few cars up track from where I stood. I boarded the carriage in front of the *fourgon* and remained in the rear vestibule until the train began to move and gather speed. I waited until it had cleared the station and the yards and was running fast along a ledge at the bottom of the limestone walls of the Ouche, before I began to make my way forward from car to car, seeking Erda.

Had she boarded? What if she had changed her mind and taken an earlier train? Or if Madame Décat had decided to accompany her to Paris? It was too late for me to don a disguise.

46

My uncertainty increased, and the sweat began to trickle down my body under my clothes, as car after car did not hold her. Passengers looked at me suspiciously as I peered into each successive compartment. The train was running at full speed now, swaying on the curves as the line climbed the low hills separating the watersheds of the Yonne and the Seine. The wintry landscape was a blur through the steamy windows. Erda, Erda, darling, darling, I kept muttering, hoping to evoke her. Although I had lost count of the cars, I knew that I was near the front of the train, for I began to hear the locomotive's exhaust, powerful and regular, overtoned by the cry of the whistle as we approached a level crossing or flew through a village. The *rapide* was due to stop only once, at Laroche-Migennes for engine water.

And then, when I had nearly given up hope of finding her, I heard my name called.

"Johnny!"

I turned. It was Erda, standing in the corridor of the first-class coach, with an older Frenchman. I had passed by the couple, not recognizing her in a black tocque, veil, tailored dark suit, a fur coat on her arm.

Relief turned to jealousy. How could she be so casual? We chatted a moment. The man regarded me as an interloper, evidently believing he had made a pickup. I grew angry. I saw his face stiffen. Erda intervened. She took my arm and said to the man, "You must say good-bye now. I am to have tea with my fiancé."

He and I bowed stiffly and I began to relax as she and I made our way back along the train.

"There *is* a restaurant car, isn't there?" she asked.

"It is in the middle of the one hundred cars that constitute this train. I had despaired of finding you and then to encounter you in the company of that *cochon!*"

"I feared you were going to strike him. I, too, had despaired of your being on the train, when you were so long in finding me. And so I let that stupid shoe salesman engage me in conversation."

"I thought I would never reach the front of the train, and

then I passed right by you without knowing it."

"Do you like me in this?"

"Lift your veil and I will tell you."

We were at table in the restaurant car. I ordered English tea, toast, and port.

"She suspected nothing," Erda exulted.

"I'll not relax until we have left the Gare de Lyon. She might have telegraphed someone to meet you and escort you to the Gare du Nord."

"It is unlikely. We will telephone my friends from the station and obtain their permission to telegraph my family in their name. They'll think it a charming deception."

I watched her remove her gloves. "Need help?"

"Later."

"You'll want me to?"

"You'll despise my woolen underwear."

"I, too, wear it in winter."

We laughed in relief and anticipation.

It was dark when we left Laroche-Migennes. The lights of villages and farms flashed by. We reached the Gare de Lyon at seven o'clock. It was swarming with passengers, brilliant with lights, noisy, confused. Would there be someone looking for her? I began to sweat again. I waited outside the P.T.T. office while she telephoned and sent the telegram to Stockholm. The Blue Train was beginning to board passengers for eight o'clock departure to the Riviera. The Simplon Orient and the Rome expresses also stood waiting.

When at last we gained a taxi and the porter stowed the bags at our feet and beside the driver and the door slammed and the car entered the traffic flow in the rainy street, I collapsed with relief. Only for a moment. I roused myself and took her in my arms and my hands went beneath her coat.

"We made it," I breathed in her ear. "Now they'll never find us."

"Oh Johnny," she murmured, turning her body to mine.

She lifted her veil. We kissed. Our mouths remained fused all the way to the hotel. My hands roamed over her body.

It was a small hotel near the Place St. Germain-des-Près.

Our large, high-ceilinged room was papered with enormous birds of paradise in red and blue. The first thing Erda did was to open one of her suitcases, dig to the bottom, extract a garment and hold it high.

"I bought it for our honeymoon," she exulted. It was a sheer black silk nightie. I took her in my arms.

"Now?"

"Isn't Johnny going to feed his girl?"

"Do you want to go out?"

"I'm hungry, and besides I want to see the boulevard at night."

And so we walked to the Place and after dining at the Restaurant des Saints-Pères, we moved across to the Café de Flore and sat on the *terrasse* next to a glowing charcoal brazier. I had never known Erda so gay and talkative. Finally she sensed my impatience.

"You want to go to bed, don't you?"

"With you. Tonight."

"Soon."

"Now."

"Isn't it nice to know we can?"

"Then let's!"

A crone hobbled up with a basket of hot chestnuts in cornucopias, freshly filled from her roaster at the corner.

"Buy me some to eat in bed," Erda teased.

Another peddler had stopped, sensing a sale, and I took a bunch of violets from his basket and pinned them on her suit lapel.

"You eat the violets," I said, "and I'll eat the chestnuts. Aren't you getting cold?"

"Poor Californian! At home this would be a mild evening."

"Shall we go now?"

"Will it be like at the fire?"

"Hotter."

"Then I'm ready."

Erda proved a vigorous lover. Her body was strong from sports and it took all my strength to lead in her clumsy ardor. When she finally fell asleep on the torn-up bed, I opened the window and looked out. Daylight had come. Snow was falling between the high buildings that lined the narrow street. The room smelled of her and me and us and violets. I lay down beside her, pulled the sheet over us, and fell asleep.

Paris in the winter, the coldest winter in years, the city shrouded in a blue-gray veil. The damp air smelled of coal smoke and Chanel. It was perfect weather only for lovers. Erda lived in delight with everything, especially the great department stores where she went shopping every afternoon. I accompanied her the first time, and then we had our first quarrel, when I said that I preferred the museums and galleries. Neither of us would yield and for the rest of the week we spent our afternoons apart, I going to the Louvre, the Luxemburg, Orangerie, Cluny, Rodin, and others I had read of and never seen. I would return to our room late afternoon with a pocketful of postcards, and soon after, Erda would burst in, laden with parcels, throw them on the floor and herself in my arms.

Then we would race to see who could be naked first, flinging our clothes around the room and falling together on the bed. Afterward I would doze and when I opened my eyes, Erda would be sitting naked on the floor, tearing open parcels and exclaiming over each thing she had bought—gifts for half of Stockholm, I teased. She always brought a gift for me—a tie or handkerchief or pen and pencil set, saving my package till the last. She was irresistible.

One day a small trunk was delivered into which she began to stow her purchases. She was like a child at Christmas, gay, responsive, and also willful and spoiled. No quarrel ever lasted for long. She would end by pulling me onto her with Viking passion. Her strength was nearly equal to mine.

Evenings found us in harmony, for each night we heard music together, feasting on riches of symphonies, chamber music, recitals, always half a dozen events to choose from.

The unbroken cold brought misery to many. Along the lower quays men and women huddled around bonfires, grotesquely wrapped in rags and newspapers against the cold. The Métro platforms were peopled with the homeless. In the Rue de Rivoli I saw a coal-wagon horse fall and snap a foreleg with a sound like a pistol shot.

We were young and in love, bearing Blake's "lineaments of gratified desire," and the suffering of others did not touch us deeply. We saw it and did not like it, but were not moved thereby; if anything, it increased our own self-absorption.

Then one morning, while we were sitting up naked in bed with café-au-lait, croissants, and confiture, Erda announced that her money was gone.

"You should have told me," I scolded her. "I have only enough to pay for our room. The rest I spent on our meals."

"Don't be cross with me, Johnny."

"But you will need money for the station and meals on the train and you're not leaving till Saturday. We must eat and we planned on chamber music tomorrow night, our last night."

She laughed. "Oh Johnny, you are so serious. Don't worry. I'll go see Sven and Gertha tonight. They'll give me money. I must go alone though."

"Why must you?"

"I just must, that's all."

"Was Sven your lover?"

"Of course not. You're the only one."

"Perhaps."

She burst into tears for the first time. "You're hateful and jealous. Why must you be?"

I embraced her. We didn't get up until noon. She had her way though. I spent a lonely evening while she went by taxi to her friends in Montparnasse. Hours passed and she did not return. I went time after time to the window, pulled the flowered drapes and looked down. Snow was falling. Taxis passed; none stopped. She did not come. I grew worried. I tried to phone. No one answered. I began to read a Tauchnitz edition of *Lord Jim*. No use. I stared at the flamboyant wallpaper and counted the birds. The bell in the tower of St. Germain struck the hours, hour after hour, and still she did not come.

It was three in the morning when she finally burst in, laden with parcels, as fresh as ever, excited and laughing.

"Don't scold me," she cried. "I have lovely presents, all for you."

"Beware of Swedes bearing gifts," I growled, half angry, half relieved.

"And money," she cried, opening her bag and flinging a handful of paper francs on the bed. "We're rich again."

"Did you sleep with Sven?"

"Johnny, you mustn't talk that way. You know I'm your girl."

"Why were you so long?"

"He insisted we go dancing, and as I'd had a thousand francs from him, I couldn't refuse."

"Why didn't you come and get me?"

She hesitated. "Well, there was another Swede there—a boy I grew up with in the Ostermalmsgatan—and Sven thought it better not to let him know I've been with you all week."

"And so the four of you went dancing."

"Don't be jealous, Johnny, please don't be."

I was not to be appeased, and for the first time we fell asleep back to back.

The morning brought another day. We awoke and turned to one another again and lay abed until early afternoon.

That last afternoon, reduced to just enough money to get her home, Erda let me lead. I took her to some of my favorite places. In the Luxembourg Museum the virility of Bourdelle's bronze Herakles Archer made her eyes shine. We walked through the bare gardens and on to St. Clothilde where César Franck had been organist, and back along the Boulevard St. Germain to the Faculty of Medicine, where I showed her the museum of monstrosities in jars of alcohol. She shuddered and clung to my arm.

We dined our last night at the Voltaire, opposite the Odéon, on trout from the Auvergne and a bottle of flowery Chablis whose bouquet brought pleasure to diners at the next table.

"I like you better poor," I toasted her. "I've had you all to myself since you came home last night."

"This morning."

"And tonight."

"Our last night."

"Don't be sad. Be glad I'm marrying a banker."

"Selling yourself."

"I gave myself to you."

"Only for a week."

"You're so serious. I thought Americans were frivolous and gay."

"Is that why you wanted to meet me?"

"Please don't be stupid."

"I want to hurt you."

"You will if you don't stop."

In spite of the food and wine, I was glum, and she gave up trying to amuse me. We took our seats in the Salle Pleyel and waited for the music to begin. We did not speak and did not hold hands. It was an all-César Franck concert, his string quartet and piano quintet. The richness of the strings brought me to life. My hand found hers.

"Oh Johnny," she whispered, leaning toward me, "isn't it beautiful?"

We were reconciled by the music to our differences and our parting. When it was over, we walked back to the hotel, seeing the great department store façades illuminated with animated toy displays for the Christmas season.

"Even if I had any money," she said, "I couldn't spend it. They're all closed."

"Do you want to stop at the Flore for a last drink?"

"Yes, and I have a confession to make."

"You mean you are?"

"I won't know that till after Christmas. Do you want me to be?"

"Would it bring you back?"

"Johnny, listen to me. I've lost my passport."

"What?"

"I must have left it in one of the shops when they asked to see my papers. I can't get through Belgium and Germany without it. What shall I do?"

It was not until we were seated at the café, with little glasses of Remi Martin, that I had an idea.

"Go to your consulate in the morning and ask for a transit passport to Sweden. They have a record of your being in France and will surely issue you one."

"They ought to, but will they?"

"Show me the man who could say no to you."

"You don't know the Swedish functionary. He's as cold as a frozen herring."

"Wear what you did coming up on the train."

"I'll try."

"Maybe he'll refuse and then you won't be able to leave."

"Be honest, Johnny. You'd grow tired of me. Or angry. You're grown up. I'm still a girl. I don't really want to settle down."

"What will *he* say about that?"

"I'll wear him out and inherit his money. Then I'll come to you."

"Mad girl!"

"You don't know how impoverished my family is. They have been living on borrowed money until my marriage is consummated. I'll wait a week, then give him a bag of bills to pay."

"Mercenary Swede. It's a horrible system."

"I don't know any other. You know now, don't you, that it's you I love."

"Are you ready for bed?"

"I'll really show you that I love you."

She did indeed. It was the best night of all. We were utterly compatible. In the fire of her surrender my destructive emotions were burned away. Delight remained in purest essence. And sleep, the deep sleep of complete fulfillment.

We rose at nine after breakfast in bed, and somehow managed to pack her things, loaded all into a cab, and drove to the Swedish consulate. I waited while she went in. I lay back in the cab, beyond feeling, and waited. The lapel of my overcoat was sweet from where her head had rested. She returned, waving a paper in her gloved hand.

"I did exactly what you said. Never lifted my veil. Removed one glove and touched his hand, oh so timidly. He issued me a transit visa—and asked me for coffee. I said no thank you, my grandfather is waiting for me." She kissed me. "Wasn't I polite?"

I leaned over the driver. He was reading *L'Ami du Peuple*. I tapped his arm.

"Alors, m'sieur 'dame?"

"Gare du Nord."

We arrived half an hour before the Hamburg *rapide* was due to depart, and after checking Erda's baggage, we entered the station buffet.

"There are shadows under your eyes," I said, "as there were that day when you came to my room."

"And for the same reason. Lack of sleep."

"I slept."

"I watched you."

"You were so good last night."

"Have I learned the American way?"

"All ways."

"Oh Johnny, you've spoiled me. You'll forget our quarrels, won't you? They were all my fault."

"Darling."

"Can you make up your work? Will Raoul aid you?"

"I'll work terribly hard to keep from thinking."

"You won't forget me?"

"Never."

"Now may I have a kümmel?"

"That's all I have left. The price of one kümmel."

"Take these francs."

"You'll need them."

"Will you go right back?"

"I hope I can make the eleven-thirty *rapide*."

"Tell the old gentleman I loved his cookies. You'll go tomorrow?"

"Every Sunday."

"I'll be listening." She raised her glass. "Skaal, Johnny." She sipped and handed me the glass.

"Skaal, Erda."

We were in the stream just above the falls.

Then we found her car, a first-class black and red Deutsches Reichsbahn carriage, with placard reading "Paris-Hamburg." Steam was billowing from between the cars. We walked forward just as the engine eased into the coupling with a soft clash of steel.

"You did that to me, Johnny," she murmured. "You did that to me."

We looked up at the gloved driver. He looked down at Erda. She blew him a kiss. "Drive carefully," she said. He looked at his watch. The air was bittersweet with the ancient smell of Paris.

Five minutes.

We walked back to her car and mounted to the vestibule. I found her beneath the fur and for the last time I ran my hands over her body. Our eyes sought the lasting image each of the other.

Two minutes.

"En voiture!" the conductor called.

Erda grimaced and wiped a tear from each eye with her gloved hand. I kissed her with all my might, until I tasted her blood in my mouth.

"Adieu," she whispered. "Good-bye, Johnny."

I kissed her again, as though I could arrest the train by the force of my desire.

Useless. The train began to move. She broke away and pushed me toward the open door. I jumped off and nearly fell. She leaned out and waved. I waved back.

The train gathered speed with incredible swiftness, and in a moment the *fourgon* glided by, faster, faster; and through a smother of steam I saw its two ruby lights, like the eyes of a beast.

III

Joyce

I spent the Christmas holidays in the laboratory, making up the lost week; and to repay the money I had borrowed, I gave English conversation lessons to French students. The cold weather endured. Streets and walks were icy and treacherous. Erda wrote twice, and sent me a copy of *Gösta Berling* in English; and though I answered and wrote again, I heard from her no more.

I was effortlessly chaste. Nothing diverted me from study. I slept late, went to the café for apéritif and lunch, was in lecture or laboratory from two until seven, dined at the *pension*, sometimes went to the movies, then returned to my room and studied and read to music, or joined in a bull session in another student's room, until going to bed long after midnight. I lived on stored-up heat from Erda. She had irradiated me for the winter.

Old Bonespoir had returned to his natal village in the Vosges and there were no more Sundays in the Rue Berbisey. I acquired my own radio receiver, and it brought in the musical riches of Europe from London to Warsaw. At my work table, which was covered with sailcloth and lighted by a lamp with an orange-colored shade, I heard music through earphones, while I labored on a translation into English of an endocrinology text by one of my research professors. Pinned on the wall above my table was a print Erda had given me, of Bourdelle's glowering bronze of Beethoven, its inscription reading, "Moi je suis Bacchus qui pressure pour les hommes le nectar délicieux."

After midnight as the stations began to go off the air, the house grew still and no sounds came from the street; then was heard only the striking of the hours on the town's many bell clocks. For the first time in my life I had broken the sensual barrier and attained a serenity in which my mind was free to flower.

And then one day in early spring when I had finished lunch

and was about to leave for the Faculty, a British couple named
Penfield entered the café. They were students of landscape
design, living in Dijon while writing a thesis on ancient
Burgundian parks. I had met them one weekend at Vézelay
where we had gone to see the Basilique de la Madeleine.
Burton Penfield was tall, thin, and bespectacled, his wife
Mildred a plump Irish woman with rose-petal skin and honey-
colored hair.

A woman was with them I had never seen before. The café
was crowded, and mine was the only table with empty seats.

"May we?" Penfield asked.

"Please do. I'll be leaving."

"Stay," Mildred Penfield said, "and meet my friend Mrs.
Davies."

The woman's eyes met mine, and I was the first to look
away. Hers were green eyes in a blank white face.

"We've been trying to persuade Joyce to see Vézelay now
that she's this close," Mrs. Penfield said, "but she insists on
going through."

"To?" I asked, to be polite.

"Cannes." Mrs. Penfield replied. "Have you been to Vézelay
again?"

"I've been too busy."

"What occupies Mr. Burgoyne so urgently?" Mrs. Davies
asked.

"Jack is a science student at the medical faculty," Penfield
said. "A slave to his studies, especially since he was in Paris
last winter."

"I do not care for doctors," the woman said.

"Jack would never actually cut into you," Penfield explained. "He's more apt to dissect you philosophically."

"Jolly brilliant, these Americans," Mrs. Penfield said.

"I would not have taken Mr. Burgoyne for an American,"
Mrs. Davies said.

"Would you like to see my passport?" I asked.

"The Americans I have known have all been rotters."

"One finds what one seeks," I said.

Our eyes met again, and this time hers dropped. She lit a

cigarette and blew the smoke in my face.

"Thanks," I said. "I happen to like the *Gauloise bleu.*"

The Penfields were embarrassed. I rose.

"Back to the formaldehyde vat," I said, "where life is less hazardous."

Mrs. Davies smiled faintly. I shook hands with all three and left.

All afternoon in the laboratory her perfume lingered on my hand, an exotic smell soap and water did not remove. I recalled her chic clothes, her long legs crossed high up, her thin face with wide mouth, and above all, her green eyes. I had not seen her hair, for she was wearing a tightly wound dark green silk turban.

I went to the movies that night to see Charlie Chaplin in *Les Lumières de la Ville.* It was the third time I had seen it, enthralled by the master pantomimist and the musical score he had composed for the picture; and I walked up the aisle afterward, humming the little flower girl's song.

Then in the crowded foyer I found myself pressed against— Joyce Davies. She was with the Penfields. When she turned to see who was crowding her, our faces nearly touched. Hers cut like a knife. Only for a moment; then her eyes widened in recognition and I saw that their green was amber-flecked.

"Monsieur le docteur," she murmured, with the faintest of smiles.

"We're going to the Miroir for coffee," Penfield said. "Will you join us?"

"Please excuse me, I said. "I have work to do."

"It would give me pleasure if you would come," Mrs. Davies said in French.

"I thought you didn't like Americans?" I countered, also in French.

"Are there not exceptions to all rules?"

"I assure you of my profoundest gratitude."

"Do come," she said in English, "I'll behave."

A whiff of her perfume decided it. I went with them up the Rue de la Liberté to the Brasserie du Miroir. A string orchestra was playing the ballet music from *Le Cid.* The

Penfields and I got into a discussion of Cluny in southern Burgundy and the merits of Viollet-le-Duc's work, while Joyce Davies listened, watching the face of each speaker, her own veiled in smoke from the strong cigarettes she favored.

"Are you always this silent?" I challenged her, in a lull of our talk.

"Afraid of angering you again."

"Joyce is still fatigued from her journey," Mrs. Penfield explained. "She came across on the Trans-Siberian."

"All the way across?" I asked. "What kind of equipment do they have?"

"Horrible. And the food was even worse. It took two weeks."

"And she wants to leave tomorrow," Mrs. Penfield said. "We are frightfully annoyed with her."

"Go on talking architecture," she said. "It's so reassuring."

She intrigued me. Who was she? Not French, although she spoke it fluently. I kept trying to place the perfume. Was it Chinese? I did not leave early as I had intended to do. It was Monday night and the Miroir and the town's other cafés all closed at eleven.

"Just as I'm waking up," Mrs. Davies protested. "Is there nowhere open that I may stand a round of Pernod?"

"The *buffet de la gare,*" I said, "is open all night."

"Shall we go there?" she asked.

"We'd better not," Penfield said. "Jack, you go with Joyce. A bit of night life will do you good."

I did not protest. And so we separated, the Penfields going off to their apartment and Mrs. Davies and I retracing the Rue de la Liberté to the Place Darcy and on to the railway station. We walked silently under an arch of plane trees in new leaf.

In the smoky buffet she removed her coat for the first time and I saw that she was a mature woman, full-breasted, round-armed, thin only in face and shapely legs.

"I see that you approve of me," she said. "I suppose you'll be wanting to sleep with me before the night is over."

I stood up in anger.

"Sorry," she said, taking my hand. "I seem to be fated to annoy you."

"You are accustomed to men finding you irresistible."

"You speak the truth."

"Have you tried not wearing that perfume?"

"I do not wear perfume."

"What is it then?"

"It is on my clothes. Our closets were made of sandalwood."

"In China?"

"Indochina."

"So that is an Oriental mask you wear."

"For protection."

"Take it off."

"Why should I?"

"Where are you staying? I'd better take you to your hotel. We don't seem to be getting along."

Her face softened. She took a long swallow of the milky Pernod. "Please don't." She lit a Gauloise. "I'm beginning to relax."

"Why so tense?"

"The long journey, I suppose. Men on the train annoyed me. There was no privacy."

"I want nothing from you."

"I'm beginning to see that you don't."

"Who are you?"

"You know my name."

"Let's not spar."

"Do you want me to take my hair down?"

"It might help."

She began to unwind the turban.

"I wrapped it too tight. It's giving me a headache."

Her hair came down in a flood, thick and curly and copper red, clear to her shoulders.

I reached out and touched it. "Will it burn me?"

She laughed. "It's all my own. Nor do I tint it."

"Why do you hide such beautiful hair?"

"I attract enough attention without this bonfire."

"It is indeed an incendiary red. Now tell me who you are."

"Please don't be an aggressive American, just as I am beginning to like you."

"Do you dislike all men at first?"

"Mostly."

"I don't suppose I'm any different from the rest. I am just a man."

"That is obvious."

"Why don't we be simple with each other? Dijon is a poor place for melodrama."

"Don't you find it dull here?"

"I do not seek excitement."

"Why are you here?"

"To work. Why are you?"

"Passing through. And to see Mildred. Do you sometimes go to Paris?"

"Not since December. The severe cold burned me."

"Your paradox fails to hide the presence of a woman."

"You are perceptive."

"Tell me about her."

"She returned to the Arctic Circle."

"Tiens, an Eskimo. How exotic!"

We laughed.

"What do you do to amuse yourself?" she asked.

"We were at the movie, remember?"

"Was that tonight?"

"Last night. We met yesterday noon."

"Do you have a girl here?"

"No."

"Lucky you. Was the one in Paris good?"

"She was really Swedish, not Eskimo."

"Where is she now?"

"She went home to Stockholm to be married."

"Lucky you."

The train caller entered the buffet and poured out a torrent of words.

"I thought I knew French," she laughed.

"He's calling the Blue Train. It's due to make a ten-minute

stop. Want to go see?"

"Whither thou goest . . ."

I put fifty-centime pieces in the vending machine for billets de quai and we gained the platform and waited beside the main line until the de luxe sleeping-car train from Calais and Paris came in precisely at midnight. Blinds were pulled on the windows of the blue and gold *wagons-lit*. A mechanic hurried along with a flashlight, crouching to check the journal boxes with a rap of his hammer. A few people boarded. No one got off. The Blue Train carried only through passengers for Marseilles and beyond.

We walked back along the train, drawn by a lighted, unshaded window. There we gazed up. Four red-faced Englishmen in shirt sleeves were sitting, rigidly erect, playing cards. We were so close that I could read the label on their bottle of Johnny Walker. One man looked down and saw us. His lips moved soundlessly. The other three turned and looked. Their faces were expressionless. We stared up at them. They turned back to their cards. The train began to move and gather speed. As the *fourgon* passed us, we saw the baggage-master standing in the open side door, his ill-fitting, red-corded, black uniform open at the throat, in the act of tilting a wine bottle to his lips.

"Santé!" I called, as the car glided past.

His Adam's apple twitched. He removed the bottle from his mouth. "À la vôtre, m'sieu'dame," he said.

Joyce squeezed my arm and laughed.

We walked the length of the platform after the departing train, until finally its rear lights disappeared around a curve. We walked out from under the shell and saw the yard signals turn red. The air was damp and smelled of coal smoke and hot oily machinery. I told her of the last times I was there and of Nancy and Erda and what I had learned from them.

Joyce clung to my arm as we walked in slow strides together and I spoke of my successes and failures. I touched her hair. It was beaded with moisture. The bitter smell of coal smoke blended with her sandalwood. We drifted back under the arch of the station.

"I call it my cathedral," I said. "Shall we eat something?"

"As you like. I seem to be yours without your asking for me."

"You've grown wonderfully gentle."

We entered the buffet and ordered ham and gruyère sandwiches, coffee and brandy.

"In a few more minutes," I said, "the Simplon-Orient is due. And then the Rome. And at 2:38 there's the Bordeaux-Strasbourg *rapide*, the only fast train in all of France that does not originate in Paris."

"I am coming to the conclusion that you like trains."

"I often come here at night to see them pass. If I do not visit the buffet, it costs only fifty centimes."

"I thought I never wanted to see a train again."

"Now tell me—are you an international spy?"

"Heavens no! The Russians took me for a whore. I might look like one, and I'm no virgin, but I've never taken money. Isn't that the definition of a whore? I would if I had to; but then I've never lacked money, so I shouldn't boast of my virtue."

"You have known many men."

"Too many."

"Is there a Mr. Davies?"

"That is my maiden name."

"You were married?"

"To a Frenchman."

"You will understand my natural curiosity about your antecedents."

"That is much nicer than 'Who are you?'"

"Our manners improve with practice."

She laughed. "My father was a Welsh adventurer, my mother an English noblewoman. He earned his living by cards and when he was blinded in an accident, he killed my mother and committed suicide. I was sent to a convent in Rouen."

"I once thought of studying there."

"It is much like Dijon though busier because of the river commerce. They are all alike, however, these provincial holes. Well, at fifteen I was seduced by a high ecclesiastic and became his mistress, until he died of apoplexy from overeating. Then I married a wealthy importer and we moved to Indochina. Ten years in Saigon and then alcohol did for him, as it will do for me, I fear. I turned down an even dozen proposals, more or less legitimate, took my maiden name, and here I am in the buffet de la gare de Dijon."

"Where do the Penfields come in?"

"Mildred was in the convent. We've kept in touch. I was curious to see if she could still excite me the way she did when we were girls."

"Does she?"

She smiled. "You didn't give me time to find out!"

"Do I excite you?"

She finished her brandy, then said, "Yes, you do."

"Are you in a hurry?"

"No. I like talking with you. There's no hurry."

"What takes you to Cannes?"

"My husband left me a villa at Antibes. I want to see whether to keep it or sell it."

"Then you are not a spy."

"You are sweet, Jack Burgoyne. Have you forgiven me?"

"For what?"

"The rude things I said."

"That was yesterday."

"Is today tomorrow?"

"It grows late. Are you tired?"

"I am not sure. Perhaps in a state of ecstatic fatigue."

"We need fresh air. Which is your hotel?"

"La Bourgogne."

"It belongs to me. I own the entire duchy of Burgundy. It was my grand-patrimony."

"May I be your first duchess?"

"Joyce the Red, all hail!"

She laughed. "I don't know which has gone most to my head—you, the brandy or the trains, but I have never been so happy. Do you learn this art at school?"

"It is the Burgundian bedside manner."

"It's your not wanting anything from me."

"Don't I?"

"Do you?"

"Your hair."

"It's not removable."

"I want to bury my face in it."

"Did you say we needed fresh air?"

"You don't want to see the other trains?"

"Not tonight." She smiled, then said, "I was wrong. I *am* in a hurry."

We went out into the damp air and walked arm in arm up the street. A group of soldiers came toward us, walking in the middle of the street, clinging together and singing drunkenly. We stopped and watched them reel past. They paid no attention to us.

"You haven't told me," she said, "that I smoke and drink too much."

"Do you?"

"Yes."

"Then that's settled."

We reached her hotel on the Place Darcy. The lobby was deserted, the room clerk snoring. We leaned against the wall at the elevator.

"Journey's end," she said, and drew my face to her hair.

We stood for a long moment. Then she opened the elevator door and held it for me.

"Will you?" she asked.

"Willingly," I replied.

We mounted to her room on the fifth and top floor. She undressed swiftly and lay on the bed and waited for me to join her.

It was nearly noon when I awoke. Joyce was still asleep, her hair like fire on the pillow. We had enjoyed long, deliberate and deeply satisfying intercourse, and I felt refreshed. I dressed quietly, and as I was about to leave without waking her, I saw her eyes open. I sat on the edge of the bed. She reached up her arms. I held her and kissed her. She laughed and fell back. On her milk white skin, her body hair was all the redder.

"I had forgotten," she said, "how good it can be."

"You'd think we'd done it for years."

67

"I wanted you the moment I saw you."

"You nearly drove me away."

"Horrible thought."

"I'm late. Will you be here after lab?"

"I was going to take the seven-thirty *rapide*."

"Don't."

"You want me to stay?"

"Yes."

"What will we do?"

"What we did."

"You want more?"

"Yes."

"So do I. Is there a quiet café where I can sit and have a drink until you come?"

"The Concorde, directly across the Place."

"It will take me until then to get the tangles out of my hair."

"Don't bother. I'll only put them back in."

When I returned at six, I found Joyce seated on the leather *banc* at the Concorde, a Pernod in front of her, a cigarette in her hand. Before she saw me, her face was expressionless as it was when we first met; and then as I approached, her eyes widened, her face relaxed, the lines disappeared and she smiled. We shook hands and I sat beside her and ordered a *demi* of Vézelise, the blonde Pilsner-type beer featured at the Concorde.

"À toi." She lifted her glass and drank it half down, then lit her cigarette and we were enveloped in a cloud of the acrid smoke.

"How is it," I asked, "that you smoke the workers' cigarette?"

"Did we not labor? The truth is, I like everything strong. You!"

"You are a strange one."

"Do you like me?"

"I haven't had time to think about it."

"Did it go well for you? Not too tired?"

"Recharged."

"I too."

"You are not leaving."

"You want me to stay?"

"You are good medicine."

Time passed as we drifted along in quiet talk, she on Pernod, I on beer, there in the peacefulness of the Café de la Concorde, its panelled, gilt-mirrored walls reflecting the older Dijonnais who frequented it as a club. Merchants and professional men and matrons, too, came for apéritifs and tea, chess, the newspapers, and talk. The waiters were old professionals, deliberate, impersonal and skilled. When ours brought more drinks, Joyce's face would resume her habitual green-eyed mask; then when he had left, she turned to me and smiled, her eyes widened and were again amber-flecked.

Toward eight she paid for the accumulation of saucers and we strolled up the Rue de la Liberté to the Place d'Armes and there at a table behind a hedge of potted privet on the *terrasse* of the Restaurant du Pré aux Clercs, we dined on steak, potatoes, salad, and Beaujolais en carafe. It was beginning to grow dark and the pigeons were settling to roost on the ledges of the Hotel de Ville, the great structure of honey-colored limestone which stood where the Dukes of Burgundy had once built their palace. The vanished rulers were symbolized by stone helmets which rose from the cornices in silhouette against the eggshell sky. A trolley car rocked crazily across the Place and disappeared down the main street with a squeal of flanged wheels.

Our waiter lit the candles on our table, and as we emptied the second carafe, Joyce took my hand across the cloth.

"Mœurs de province," she said. "Bearable only when one knows they are not permanent, that one can escape them."

"But not tonight."

"Not tonight."

I held her knee between my knees; our hands too were joined.

"When?" I asked.

"Let us live each day."

"And night."

"Again so soon?"

"It was long ago."

"We met only yesterday."

"A century ago."

"You are unusually romantic for one studying the sciences."

"You have heard of Arthur Schnitzler? Of Somerset Maugham? Of James Joyce?"

"I have small culture and large appetite."

"I will teach you."

"You have."

We strolled back up the street to her hotel. It was now dark and the bright shop windows offered beautiful displays of mustard jars, gingerbread, and confections, Dijon's specialties on view for the passerby. A soft spring rain was falling as we turned in and again mounted to her room. There we opened the tall windows that looked across a courtyard with elms and chestnuts in leaf to the cathedral of St. Bénigne. The air smelled strong of wet earth, sandalwood and tobacco. Our lips tasted of wine as we stood at the open window in a searching kiss, hearing the sound of rain on the leaves.

And thus a week went by, each day and night the same for us. We met at the Concorde, dined at the Pré aux Clercs, walked up the street to her hotel, stood at the open window and kissed, undressed and made love. Each morning I went away refreshed to the day's work at the Faculty. There were no variations in the slow and muted music that we made. I was not in love as I had known it before, nor even infatuated. When we met in the afternoon, it was as friends, and it was not until we had finished dinner and were holding hands across the table, our knees gripped together, relaxed, assured; and I saw her peaceful, smiling face, that I began to feel desire again.

"Shall we go now?"

"It's lovely not being in a hurry."

"I am now."

"So am I. Go and I will follow."

The Penfields called us a stuffy old married couple. Our sole concession to sociability was to go with them one evening to the movie—René Clair's *Sous les Toits de Paris.*

"Those train whistles," Joyce said, as we talked after love.

"They'll haunt me forever."

"He used them as a leit-motif."

"They'll be ours. That first night at the station! Those Englishmen! I've never known enchantment like this."

"Listen, you can hear the yard engines."

"And the rain on the leaves. Oh Jack, it's too good to last."

I kissed her words away.

Sunday afternoon we walked to the park on the only fine day since she had come. It was the first time I had been there since the winter walk with Erda. Now the trees made a green sky overhead. Thrushes sang. A cuckoo called. Children rolled hoops down the smooth walks. We reached the riverbank and sat on the stone bench. Across the stream the grassy field was the nesting place of larks and they rose up singing.

"I was reading Henry James's *Little Tour in France*," I said, "and it's here on this very bench that he brings it to a close. He did not like Dijon."

"He was probably alone. I'd go mad if I were here alone. I'll remember it because of you."

"You sound sad."

"Nostalgic, I guess, remembering Sunday afternoon walks along the river in Rouen. Now I'll add Dijon to memory."

"What are you telling me?"

"That I'll be leaving."

"No."

"You didn't think I'd stay forever."

"But it's only been a week."

"I intended to stay only a day."

"We could pool our money and share an apartment."

"Money's not the problem."

"What is?"

"You. You are losing weight. You can't go on with such a regime. What you have been lavishing on me belongs to your work."

"I have enough for both. I have never felt better."

"Nothing in excess, my husband used to say when I began on the second bottle of Pernod."

"I've never known one like you. You do not keep me aroused."

"I take that as a compliment."

"Stay. We'll find an apartment tomorrow."

"Now you're being that aggressive American. Don't forget, I've loved you because you weren't one."

"Be reasonable."

"I am. Oh Jack, you've been the first who's not sought to reform me. I truly have bad habits and a worse character."

"We have had other things to do."

"Lovely things, and all lovely things do pass. You're poet enough to know that."

"I refuse to be categorized."

She stood up.

"Let's walk. Talking is not good for this afternoon."

She had her way. We wandered back through the park, then returned to town along the riverbank and the canal path, past the hospital and the Faculty and the workers' quarter in the Rue Monge and the statue of Bossuet preaching, a fat pigeon on his head. I showed her a secret garden behind the stone wall of a deserted hotel. There against the side of the building was a well-shrine, with a stone cupid and the inscription "Tout par amor, 1539." Lilacs had grown wild, the bushes were covered with purple blossoms, the air sweet with their fragrance.

"I could have loved you well," she said. "Why was it not you who came over the convent wall?"

We reached the Place Émile Zola as the fanfare of the P.L.M. began its Sunday afternoon concert—a dozen middle-aged railway workers in sloppy blue and red uniforms, blowing blasts of strident music. We found a table on the *terrasse* of the tiny Café du Midi. The leafy square was thronged with promenading Dijonnais. Children had scrambled atop the iron *pissoir* and were gaping over the crowd at the sweating musicians. We drank warm beer from green bottles. It was a spectacle Breughel would have relished. The music and shouting, barking dogs and roaring motorcycles made conversation impossible.

When it grew dark we walked on to the Pré aux Clercs for dinner. The Place d'Armes was also peopled with promenaders, the quieter bourgeoisie, and behind the hedge we were able to talk again.

"It's a poem by Rimbaud," I said. "Listen!"

Les tilleuls sentent bon dans les bons soirs de juin.
L'air est parfois si doux qu'on ferme la paupière.

"Where was he when he wrote that?"

"Charleville."

"The dreary north. What escapists you poets are! If I shut my eyes, I'm back in Rouen. Oh Jack, why did it have to be the way it was?"

"Stay and we'll make it over."

"An old drunkard like me? Besides, you're my last man. I intend to live with women after this. Anyway, I'll be dead of lung cancer before I'm forty. Look at my fingers. You'd think I was Chinese. What could I give you? A child? No. The good father took care of that. He told me it was an appendectomy when he destroyed my ability to bear a child. My best gift to you would be my body in alcohol."

"Don't talk like that. You never have before."

"You're hearing the true me. I've hidden her for a week, thanks to you. Now you must face her, you fool."

"Please be reasonable."

"A lovely week for me. I've gained the weight you've lost. The lines are gone from my face. My hair is glossy again."

"Green eyes turned amber."

"You haven't asked anything of me. For God's sake, don't start now."

"Only that you stay for a while."

"You are a damn fool, John Burgoyne."

She began to laugh hysterically and I realized that for the first time she was drunk. I went across the square to the carriage stand, came back for her and we drove to the hotel. There she was quiet, and when we were in bed, she was violent in love, and then lay exhausted. It was nearing eleven when she pushed me gently out of bed.

"Go," she said. "Let us both get a good sleep."

She watched me dress, and then when I was putting on my

shoes, she knelt naked and tied the laces. I buried my face in her hair, as she hugged my knees. Sandalwood, tobacco, wine, and woman were blended in one strong perfume. I drew her up and held her against me.

"You will stay?"

"Yes, but go now. I'm so tired."

"Tomorrow?"

"Oui, à demain. Va t'en, mon amour. Laisse-moi dormir."

She pushed me into the hall and I heard the door lock.

All the next day I was impatient to see her. It was the first time I had not been able to concentrate on my work. On my way to the Concorde I bought a nosegay of lilies of the valley—porte bonheur—the first time I had taken her flowers.

She was not in the café. I crossed the Place to the hotel. The room clerk stared when I asked him to ring Madame Davies.

"She has left."

"What?"

"She is no longer here."

"Do you mean that she has checked out?"

"That is the fact."

"Since when?"

"She left last night, soon after you did."

"Where has she gone?"

"She said that she was taking the *de luxe* at midnight."

"The Blue Train?"

"That's the one. For the Côte d'Azur. Some people have all the luck. They say it is fine weather down there."

"Doubtless. But did not Madame leave a message for me?"

"She left nothing at all, save the scent of a strange perfume."

"She was alone?"

"But certainly."

I thrust the lilies into my pocket and left the hotel. It had begun to rain. I crossed the square to the Concorde and sat down on the *banc*. The old flat-footed garçon came for my order.

"Monsieur desires?"

"The usual."

"Shall I bring Madame's?"

"She will not be here."

The waiter peered at me, then elaborately wiped off the marble-topped table with his towel.

"Then you are alone," he concluded.

"That, alas, is the exact truth. She took the Blue Train last night."

"I am truly sorry to hear that. You made a brave couple."

"That's life, my friend."

"True. One learns from experience that it is not all roses."

IV

Madeleine

The rainy spring merged into a rainy summer. The vintage failed. A cold wind blew from the east. The natives groaned.

I never heard from Joyce. The Penfields reported that she had sold the villa in Antibes and gone they knew not where.

I finished my studies and received my degree in early autumn. As my two-year fellowship had ended, I prepared to return to the United States and seek a laboratory appointment in or near San Francisco. Then one afternoon I received a letter from a legal firm in San Diego, transmitting a draft for $2,000, drawn on the Dijon branch of the Société Générale. It was the residue of my mother's estate, the very last of her gifts to me; and it decided me to stay on in Europe until it was gone. From all accounts, prospects of employment even for trained scientists were bleak. The Depression was becoming worldwide.

I hoped to write a book for which I had long been reading and making notes, a book on tuberculosis and art, studied in the works of Keats, Stevenson, Katherine Mansfield, and D. H. Lawrence. The latter two had died in France, and the first step would be to go to the south of France where Lawrence had lived his last days and to Italy where he had written *Lady Chatterley's Lover*. There I planned to interview doctors who had treated him and to soak up local color.

I was starved for sun. The golden limestone of the ducal city had lost its glow and gone gray. Dijon had become a morgue of grim weather. And so I closed my small affairs, said my good-byes, and on my last afternoon I called a taxi, stowed my bags therein, and drove to the bank on the Place du Théâtre. There I cashed the draft and took the fifty crisp new thousand-franc notes, folded and buttoned them down in an inner pocket of my coat. They gave me a feeling of great wealth.

Next, I directed the driver to the station, where I checked my baggage through to Nice on the seven-thirty *rapide*. Then I walked back the length of the main street to the Café de

Paris, where I had first seen Erda pass and had met Joyce, said good-bye to the frog-faced proprietor and the waiters, and had a *porto sec* on the house. Then I paid homage to the bronze statue of Jean-Philippe Rameau, and in the courtyard of the Hotel de Ville to that of Claus Slüter, the Flemish sculptor, *imagier aux ducs*, standing aproned in the rain, his mallet and chisel upraised. I thought of them as friends.

Finally I climbed the circular staircase of the stone tower to the lookout platform for a last view over the town. In vain. Rain mist hid all but the nearest buildings, their multicolored tile roofs shining wet, their myriad chimney pots asmoke. Almost directly below was the Place d'Armes and the Pré aux Clercs where Joyce and I had dined every night for a week, its *terrasse* deserted, tables and chairs taken in for the winter.

Back on the main street I retraced my steps to the Place Darcy and entered the Concorde for a last *demi* of Vézelise. The old garçon approached, towel on arm.

"Monsieur desires?"

"The same." And when he returned with deliberate tread, carefully wiped the foaming glass and set it on the cardboard coaster, I declared, "You have worked here a long time."

"It will soon be thirty-seven years."

"I leave now. This is my last drink with you."

"I read in the *Progrès* that you completed your studies with honor."

"I have been fortunate here. It was a milieu that suited my temperament."

"It astonishes me that you endured our weather."

"It does not improve."

"It has become absolutely vicious. No spring, no summer, no vintage, and now the Gastronomic Fair is threatened. Soon we shall be entering the Ark."

"They say one enjoys fair weather on the Côte d'Azur. I leave for Nice on the seven-thirty."

"If this proves to be true, I beg of you to dispatch us some of their weather." He drew closer and lowered his voice, employing the subjunctive. "If it should not be indiscreet of me to ask, would you be rendezvousing with Madame?"

"You remember her?"

A slow smile spread over his moon face. "But certainly! She did not walk as an ordinary woman walks, but rather with a serpentine motion."

"That is well put, my friend. She was unusually supple."

He looked thoughtful. "You were fortunate in her company."

"I do not forget her, although let me say in all frankness, hers is not a troubling memory."

"It is curious, but I could never identify the perfume she wore."

"It was sandalwood. Her garments were permeated with it from having been hung in closets made of that wood."

"That is extraordinary. Certainly not here in France."

"In Indochina. In Saigon, to be exact."

"What you tell me is truly exotic. Does one enjoy such encounters in your country?"

"Hardly."

"I sometimes fancy that her fragrance lingers here where she sat with you so often."

"You are truly a man of sensitive perceptions."

"It is my métier. One learns from observing people."

I paid. We shook hands.

I went on to the station and dined in the buffet on steak, potatoes, salad, and a *demi-carafe* of Beaujolais. My sense of well-being was boundless.

The *rapide* was on time, its carriages shining from the rain, the couplings billowing steam. I boarded and found an unoccupied first-class compartment. Rain was falling as we left the shelter of the station, and I saw only a blur of lights through the streaming window. I pulled the shade, switched on the blue light, removed my shoes and coat and stretched out on the long seat with my overcoat for blanket. Soon I heard the wheels going over the switch-points at the Swiss junction and I knew we were on the main line south, via the Rhone Valley and Lyon, to the Côte d'Azur.

It was a smooth ride and I slept through the night. When I awoke we were somewhere east of Marseilles, running fast

through low hills forested with pine and oak and a heather-
like scrub, yielding to terraced olive orchards. The day was
clear, and I knew the weather was warm by sight of the
peasants in the fields, stripped to the waist. From Cannes to
Nice the train followed the shore. I saw white sails on the
water and the colored stucco villas. It was the Blue Coast at
last.

My destination was the fishing village of Cros de Cagnes,
eight miles west of Nice, where the *pension* called Le Soleil
had been recommended by my professor of endocrinology as
an unfashionable place of simple comfort and good food. The
proprietor, Monsieur Torquet, met me at Nice with an old
Citroën carryall. We loaded my bags, he picked up foodstuffs
at the wholesale market, and we headed for home.

"As one of our dear friend's students," the proprietor said,
"I shall ask you to look at my mother. A sad case, just home
from hospital in Nice with what is declared to be a terminal
case of cancer."

"I am not a medical doctor."

"Nevertheless, I should value your opinion as to the prob-
ability of her surviving through the year."

"I am at your service."

The Soleil stood on the beach, a few hundred yards west of
the post office, café, general store, and huddle of fishermen's
houses that constituted the village. It was a three-story, faded
yellow stucco building with a pink tile roof. I was given a
front room on the top floor, overlooking the pebbled beach
and the sea and along the coast in each direction. The few
guests were French. The English tended to resort in Cannes or
Nice; the Americans preferred old Cagnes on the hill in back
of the beach.

The Torquet family of several generations staffed the
pension, and I was asked by the proprietor to look at the old
grandmother even before I had unpacked my bags. The entire
family gathered around while I stood by her bed. She was
stupified with morphine. Her heart was strong, her handclasp
powerful. She would probably live thus until the malignant
growth on the neck closed her windpipe.

"There is no hope at all, they told us at the hospital," the son whispered.

I nodded in agreement.

"Her room has a view of the maritime Alps," he said. "Mama enjoyed it more than that of the sea. Now she is indifferent, but we leave her here. I must apologize for the smell. Bandaging the dying flesh seems to do no good."

"It is only natural," I said, "when one approaches the end from such a malignancy. Keep her free of pain. That is all that remains. Is that not the main line of the P.L.M.?"

"You came along it this morning. There are good walks beyond it, if you care for such."

"I have a hunger for earth under my feet. They have become calloused from the cobbled streets of Dijon."

They gave me a small study in a summer house in the *pension's* garden; and there I spread out books and notes and spent my mornings in bliss. Before lunch I walked along the beach road to the café, and at an outdoor table under a trellised grapevine, I took an apéritif of the local white wine, mild and slightly sour, and nibbled on the plate of olives that was always served. On the beach across the road, the fishermen's women sat mending nets. The sun was warm, the sea blue and without surf or tide. The flora recalled California: bougainvillea and oleander, the trees of orange and lemon, olive, eucalyptus and pepper, mimosa and persimmon.

I led an idyllic life, at peace in body and mind. Evenings were spent in the *pension* parlor, gossiping with family and guests, listening to the radio, or reading *L'Eclaireur de Nice et du Sud-Est*. Several Frenchwomen came and went. They might have been my sisters for all the effect they had on my senses.

The autumn became winter, as at home, without any perceptible change of weather. The *pension* was absurdly cheap. I foresaw no change until early summer when I planned to move on to Florence.

Then one windy afternoon of early spring I was on the beach in front of the *pension*, practicing a boyhood sport recalled since coming to the Cros. The strand was composed of egg-size, varicolored igneous pebbles brought down from the Alps by the River Var which emptied into the Mediterranean a few miles east of the village. From two strings of rawhide and a leather pocket obtained from the village shoemaker, I fashioned a sling; and standing on the shore I hurled pebbles at targets along the verge or floating in the water. It was an old sport from which I derived pleasure.

On this particular afternoon when I was pegging away at a partly submerged crate, I felt eyes on me. I turned. A woman was watching me, seated out of the wind with her back against a blue dory. I had not seen her when I came out. She was not one of the *pensioners*. She wore a heavy coat and a red scarf around her black hair. She looked more Italian than French. I finally looked away and turned to walk farther on.

"Don't stop," she called, "I beg of you. You throw beautifully, like a young David."

I walked away without answering, resentful at having my sport interrupted. I was wearing old clothes, and from her allusion, I believed she had taken me for a shepherd from the hills. I walked westward along the beach to a grove of umbrella pines called La Pinède which sheltered another *pension;* and there, beyond her sight, I resumed my slinging.

When I came down for dinner that evening, she was there, seated alone at a corner table, eating with a book in one hand. I felt my face turn red. She did not look up, nor did she gaze my way during the meal. After my embarrassment had passed, I observed her closely. She was beautiful, with creamy skin, black hair braided around her head, a long Greek nose, high forehead, full mouth with curving red lips, long lobed ears set with tiny red drops. An actress, I surmised, come for a secluded rest. I remember her voice, free of the coarse accent which characterizes the speech of the south-eastern French. For the first time since Joyce had gone, I felt a quickening of emotion. Or was it merely remembrance of my rudeness on the beach?

She finished eating before I did, and gathering a shawl around her shoulders, she walked to the front door and left without looking my way. She moved with ease and grace, a small woman with slim legs and little feet, a mature woman of poise and elegance.

Instead of reading the *Éclaireur* and conversing, I walked to the café and enjoyed a cognac. I returned in an hour, hoping that I might find the newcomer with the family and be introduced. She was not there, nor did she return. I kept from asking about her, and finally gave up and went to my room.

I did not see her in the morning or at lunch. Perhaps she had come and gone. I could have asked. I did not. The current that bore me was languid.

I went for a walk after lunch, striking back across the railroad and the highway into the hills, bushed with wild lavender in flower. I broke off a bunch and tied it to my belt like an enormous sachet. Then I worked my way up and back to the low summit of the first range and there I rested, seeing below me the white-walled farmhouses, red-roofed and blue-shuttered, surrounded by vineyards and olive orchards. Brimming cisterns gleamed amid clumps of dark pines. I could hear the chop-chop of hoes, the sounds of children at play and barking dogs, and a man's high voice singing a folk song. Down below from where I had come, the blue sea was molded like a mirror to the shore. In the west I could see the Esterel range beyond Cannes. I stretched out and dozed.

The sun was nearly set when I started home. I passed terraced fields of night-blooming jasmine where peasant women were watering the plants. They would return before sunrise and harvest the flowers for the perfume factories at Grasse.

It was twilight when I reached the railroad back of the village. The northbound Blue Train was due to pass through at five forty-five. I was used to hearing it each evening as I washed up for dinner, flying by with a shriek of its whistle.

Now I leaned on the lowered crossing-gate and waited. In the half-light the tiny station was almost hidden by an enormous purple bougainvillea. Then the rails began to hum. The train was coming. I felt my skin prickle with gooseflesh. The whistle sounded, and suddenly there it was, drawn by the great black engine with copper-banded boiler gleaming in the fading light. Like a mad angel the train swept by, the blue and yellow *wagons-lit* with lighted windows and blurred faces. The red lights of the *fourgon* glared back, then vanished around the curve of track. I heard the whistle, wailing for the next village, and the diminishing sound of rolling wheels on iron rails. There remained a light pall and smell of coal smoke. And silence. My heart was pounding.

The old crossing guard hobbled out to raise the barrier. He saw me still leaning on it, and muttered a *bon soir*.

"It really rolls," I said, with a gesture down track.

"I should think so," he croaked. "It's making eighty when it passes here. They say it makes a hundred before it reaches Cannes." He tugged on the wheel and the barrier slowly rose. "They eat well, I'm told, and they sleep together. What follies those passengers enjoy!" He rubbed his hands together, chuckled, and crept back in to his meal.

It was that evening after dinner that I met her. Her name was Mademoiselle Montrechet. We remained in the family group at first, and then as they settled into their routines of cards and sewing, she and I withdrew to a wicker settee in a corner of the parlor.

"You are not still annoyed with me?" she asked.

"Was I ever?"

"Yesterday when I drove the young David from his favorite place."

"I believed you took me for a yokel. I regret the rudeness I displayed."

"It was I who was forward."

"Did you know I was a *pensioner*?"

"Of course. The little hunchback slavey pointed you out to me before I went to the shore."

"Emma is a beastly gossip. I have had to forbid her to interrupt my work."

"I would not have taken you for an American."

"They say my French blood shows."

"Only an American, however, would think of making sport with a sling. It impressed me as infinitely droll."

"I am not used to performing for an audience." I paused. "Nor such a beautiful one."

"Are all Americans such flatterers?"

"I do not see people in nationalistic terms. I see them first as human beings. I see you first as a woman. But I confess, I do not know your nationality, and I am curious."

"Let me test your cleverness."

"Are you Italian?"

"It is true that I am often taken for such because of my features and complexion. Actually, I am French. My mother is of Pau in the Basses-Pyrenées, my father Parisian, a professor of history. I was born in Paris, but I often go to Pau and its environs."

"Then you must have Basque blood or Spanish."

"I myself have never been beyond the borders of France."

"Do you know Burgundy?"

"Only the Morvan. My father directed researches there in pre-Roman Gaul. I used to go with him when I was little. There are many Celtic traditions to be found there, as well as menhirs and dolmens."

"And Vézelay?"

"Very well. A most beautiful sanctuary."

"If I may ask without being indiscreet, are you an actress?"

"Heavens no! Why would you think that?"

"Because of your beauty and your way of carrying yourself. Do not think me forward if I say that I felt an urge last evening to rise and follow you out."

She laughed. "Do you flatter all women this way? I must consult Emma."

"I have been a recluse for months. Tell me though, are you not connected with the arts?"

"Are all Americans as curious as you, or is it something you learned in your studies?"

"My interest *is* in research."

"And you regard me as raw material!"

"Don't say that. But you are a wonderful specimen."

"I assure you of the regularity of my natural functions."

"I have already taken your pulse."

"Without holding my wrist?"

"From the artery that throbs in your neck."

"Is it poetry that you write in the summerhouse?"

"No, but I am a devoté of the Symbolists. Myself, I am writing another kind of work."

"Do you ever read it aloud? My English needs practice."

"I might be persuaded." I paused. "You are the first woman I have talked with in a long time."

"I am honored."

"I do not mean it that way."

"What do you mean?"

"I feel drawn to you by instinct. Do not misunderstand me. I have no carnal motive."

She laughed. "You are a man. All men are carnal. Therefore . . ."

"Do not tease me."

"I do not tease you, my friend, but you say and do things that afford me vast amusement."

"Have you been here before?"

"Each year on holiday."

"You work then."

"Yes, I work."

"May I ask at what?"

"You are also a persistent man. I will tell you. I am a journalist. I am on the staff of *L'Œuvre*."

"I used to read it occasionally, but not since I have been here. *L'Éclaireur* is the local bible."

"I read no papers when I am on holiday."

"You live in Paris."

"Do you like my city?"

"Not in December. I am a southerner. I will visit you in Pau. I have never seen your Southwest."

"Why did you come to France?"

"Primarily to engage in endocrinological research. I had a fellowship."

"Then you are a doctor of medicine?"

"Of science. I was a medical student at home but gave it up to come to France."

"Why did you discontinue that line of study?"

"It was my father's wish that I follow him as an M.D. He

died when I was in my teens. I sought to carry out his wish, and until my mother died two years ago, I did so, successfully—and unhappily. Her death left me free, and also with a small income. I determined to study pure science in the land of my ancestors."

"They say physicians are badly needed in your country."

"I am lacking in social conscience."

"You are an individual. That is what brought you home to France."

"I had tired of the group life we led as students. Here in France one is left alone."

"That is indeed our character."

"I thrived in Dijon, but once my degree was granted and I received a small inheritance, I came to this milder climate."

"Jean de Bourgogne is now Jean de la Côte d'Azur. Do you practice any of the arts?"

"I paint."

"Here?"

"Once in the refectory at the Faculty."

"An odd place for such."

"We painted the goddess of love under diagnosis by the class. All of us were involved in a kind of Burgundian Rembrandt."

"What was your part in it?"

"I painted a wart on her rump."

She laughed. "How very droll you are!" She looked at her wrist watch. "It grows late. I must go. We have talked at such length!"

"I ended up talking instead of asking."

"I must say good-night to my sister."

"Is she here with you?"

"She is with friends at La Pinède."

"May I accompany you?"

"Please, no."

She left again by the front door.

Although I saw her after dinner on succeeding nights, she was reserved. Had I been too bold? Had my eyes showed the hunger she stimulated in me? Though I was attracted by her, I also sensed that she did not welcome ardent attention. Each evening after we had talked awhile, she excused herself to say good-night to her sister. I managed to restrain my curiosity and cool my ardor.

Then one evening she went to her room after dinner and returned with a book. It was *Lady Chatterley's Lover*, in English.

"I bought it in Nice today," she said. "My friends in Paris have been talking about it. Will you help me over some of the difficult parts? My English is so slight."

"Do you know how naughty it is?" I teased.

"How so? The subject is love, is it not? Is that regarded as naughty in your country?"

"That depends on who does the loving."

"Just so."

She read aloud where we sat in the corner, haltingly with a thick accent, I helping her to pronounce and to translate. The parlor thinned out until at last we were alone. It was the first night she had not gone to La Pinède. At ten-fifteen we put down the book and heard the B.B.C. news from London.

"This Mellors," she said when the broadcast was over, "he is not like any Frenchman I have known. Do you as an American understand his psychology?"

"I don't know what you mean 'as an American.' As a man, yes, I do. His wanting to remain aloof. I have felt that way. I do feel that way. Or do I?" My eyes sought hers. She turned her face. They she spoke again.

"A strange thing, this love out-of-doors. Lawrence seemed to have a passion for it."

"We love nature more than you do. I wish you would come with me for a walk in the hills. They are so beautiful now with the lavender in bloom. I am going again to Vence where Lawrence is buried to visit the sanitarium where he died. I need to copy his chart to use in my book. Go with me, I beg of you."

"I must be with my sister."

"Is she ill?"

"I can only say that she needs me."

She rose. I saw that she was troubled. She said good-night and went to her room.

I was puzzled. My life was so well ordered that I was reluctant to become involved, and apparently she felt the same. And yet we were mutually attracted.

I made the pilgrimage to Vence, found Lawrence's grave, and met the physician who had attended him in his last illness. He allowed me to copy the chart. There had not been an autopsy.

Back on the beach at day's end, triumphant at the success of my quest, I broke a spray of bloom from the mimosa tree in front of the *pension*. The pollen-heavy fragrance excited me. I wanted her to smell it. She was at table when I came in. My heart pounded. I gave her the little branch. She smelled it, then looked at me curiously.

"From his grave?"

"From the tree of life. It is for you. Breathe its fragrance. Drink one of the golden balls in your wine. You will live forever."

"What makes you so fantastic this evening?" Her eyes widened.

"You do." Her eyes dropped. "May we talk later?" I dreaded her reply. She looked up.

"Yes," she said. "I'd like that."

Our eyes held for a long moment. Then I went to wash up. I stared in the mirror. The current had quickened.

We sat later on the settee while the parlor hummed around us. I was tongue-tied for the first time, afraid to speak lest I reveal my desire. Again she read from *Lady Chatterly* and we talked about Lawrence and my day.

Then the B.B.C. came on. "This is London," the distant voice spoke. We were alone. The others had retired, not caring for news in English.

Then for the first time I felt the heat of her leg next to mine. She must have sensed my awareness, for her body suddenly changed. What circuit had been joined? Had the mimosa proved a love charm? Or could it be Lawrence's ghost, drawn by her voice? Whatever it was, I knew that we had come together after touch and go; and in that moment of revelation, I sought to control my trembling body, while the calm voice recounted the world's woe. My hand sought hers and closed over it. Now it was she who trembled. The news ended. The Mayfair Hotel dance band came on, playing "Penthouse Serenade."

I stood and held out my hand. She rose and I took her in my arms, and we moved slowly over the blue and white linoleum floor among the empty tables and chairs. I held my body away from hers. Only my hand, resting lightly on the small of her back, felt the warmth of her flesh, and my cheek next to her hair knew its softness. I breathed her fragrance, a perfume faint and delicate. The music quickened into "Sailing on the Robert E. Lee," and round and round we moved in tempo.

When it ended, she disengaged herself and went out the front door. Was she bound for La Pinède? I waited a moment, then followed. She was leaning against the trunk of the mimosa tree, the tree of life. The charm, the charm! A full moon cast a glittering track over the water. Her body was arched against the tree, her face uplifted to the moon like a priestess. The air was redolent with mingled scent of mimosa, eucalyptus, rose-geranium, and sea wrack. The only sound was of the little waves of the tideless sea, breaking softly on the shingle. The night was enchanted. I stood close, so that our knees touched.

"Aren't we getting behind in our reading?" she asked, matter of fact.

The spell was broken. She had run outdoors to break it. I leaned away.

"We are like Paolo and Francesca," I said. "Dante tells how they were reading together in the garden, and when they came to a certain passage, they turned and kissed and read no more that day."

"How persuasive you Americans are!"

"I am only a man."

"How persuasive you men are! But my arms are cold. I go in."

I followed. She was not in the parlor. I went upstairs. Her

room was also on the top floor at the back of the *pension*, overlooking the mountains. A light shone from under her door. I knocked. She opened it.

"Madeleine," I pleaded. It was the first time I had used her name. "Madeleine, dear one, don't run away. Come to my room. There is a marvelous passage in Lawrence I want to read to you. Not in *Lady Chatterley*. It is in another of his books, one that I bought in Nice. Come and hear."

She allowed me to lead her by the hand, and we tiptoed down the dark hall. We heard footsteps below, and then a door shut softly. We stood listening. In a moment the stink of death drifted up to us. The son had given his mother her eleven o'clock injection. Madeleine shuddered and clung to me. I led her into my room and locked the door.

She stood by the lukewarm radiator. All I could offer in the way of refreshment was an apple. She bit into it, then handed it to me to bite. In a moment I read from *Apocalypse:*

What man most passionately wants is his living wholeness and living unison, not his own isolate salvation of his 'soul.' Man wants his physical fulfilment first and foremost, since now, once and once only, he is in the flesh and potent. For man, the vast marvel is to be alive. Whatever the unborn and the dead may know, they cannot know the beauty, the marvel of being alive in the flesh. We ought to dance with rapture that we should be alive in the flesh, and part of the living incarnate cosmos.

"That is beautiful the way you read it," she said, when I put the book down. "I am not sure I understand it all, but I won't ask you now to make a translation."

"You see it was not a deception. I *did* want to read to you."

I took the apple core from her and put it on the table. Then I stood facing her. She looked at me quizzically, as if to ask, how came we here? She was so beautiful that I could not keep from reaching out my hand and caressing her bare arm. Her eyes spoke to me. My arm went around her waist. I found her eager to be kissed.

We leaned against the radiator in that first long embrace. But when I grew bold, she gently freed herself, unlocked the door and slipped away. I followed and tried her door. It was locked.

I went back to my room, my body alert and glowing. I undressed and stood naked on the balcony. From beyond the village came the coughing roar of an African lion. A little ambulatory circus had arrived that day and pitched its caravan on the shore. I gradually cooled off, then chilled, and went to bed. Sleep came quickly.

I did not see her all the next day. She did not come down for lunch. I knocked on her door afterward. No answer. I tried the knob. Locked. I walked along the beach past La Pinède, as far as the willow-grown mouth of the Cagnes. I did not see her. Had she left? I feared to ask. My mind kept turning over each detail of the night before. What had I done to drive her away? All I could think of was Madeleine Montrechet.

After returning from the walk I sat blankly over my notes in the sunroom. The door opened. It was Emma, the slavey.

"I thought perhaps your basket needed emptying."

"It is as empty as I."

The little hunchback sidled closer. "What troubles you, Monsieur Jean?"

"Have you seen Mademoiselle?"

Her beaked face opened in a gold-toothed grin. "You're lovesick," she cackled.

"Answer me."

"Not since breakfast."

She fingered the edge of the table with a claw hand, then looked up, half sly, half wistful.

"Do you think she is beautiful?" she asked.

"Very."

"And desirable?"

"Utterly."

"And I? I am ugly. Is it not so?"

"Everyone loves you, little witch that you are."

"But no one wants to sleep with me. Only those stinking

fishermen, so drunk they don't know who I am."

I laid my hand on her lank black hair, but she broke away, sobbing, and scuttled out the door.

I walked to the café later and drank a *chopine* of white wine that raised my spirits. When she did not appear for dinner, I despaired again. At eight o'clock there was a broadcast from Prague of the *Bartered Bride*. I pulled my chair close to the loud-speaker and sought solace in Smetana's joyous music.

During the first entr'acte, as I sat with my face bent over in my hands, I heard the front door open. I peered through the bars of my fingers. It was Madeleine, hair wind-blown, cheeks flushed, eyes sparkling. I rose eagerly. She greeted me impersonally and took a hand of cards from one of the family.

Her face told me nothing. She laughed and was gay. I closed my eyes and returned to the music.

Ten o'clock came and still she played cards. Finally she rose and came over to the radio. I stood up.

"Bonne nuit," she said, holding out her hand.

I took it. A note transferred to mine. After she had left the room, I sat down with my back to the parlor, unfolded the note and read it.

"Come to my room, if it pleases you."

I could hardly sit through the London news. At ten-thirty I went to my room, took a sponge-off, donned robe and slippers, and stepped out on my balcony. Again the glitter lay on the water. The fishing fleet was scattered darkly over the bay. I breathed a prayer to Diana and went to Madeleine's room.

She answered my knock in a soft voice. I entered. She sat at the dresser with her back to me, brushing her long hair. Our eyes met in the mirror. Her face was grave. I went to the back of her low bench and stood. Her fragrance dizzied me. I laid my hands on her shoulders. She wore a thin blue silk kimono which did not insulate the heat of her body. She continued to brush her crackling hair.

"You wanted to come?" she asked.

I buried my face in her hair. She laid down the brush.

"Did you look for me today?"

"I thought you had gone."

"I had to go to Nice. I longed for you, my love, dear Jean."
It was the first time she had called me that. "I feared you
would be angry at my running away last night, like a foolish
girl. I had to. I was not well."

She rose, still facing the mirror. "Tonight I am well."

Her kimono opened and and she let it slide to the floor. I
saw her body in the glass, the rosy-nippled breasts, the love
hair a dense black against the ivory of her skin.

I let my robe fall to the floor, turned her gently to face me,
took her in my arms and carried her to the bed.

When finally we lay side by side, she said, "I have never
loved an American before. Am I as good as the women of
your country?"

"You have had my virginity."

She laughed. "Do you like me?"

"Do you seek another proof?"

"In a moment, but first, let me hear you say it."

"From the very first sight, sitting there out of the wind,
black hair, red scarf, blue boat."

"You wondered?"

"No. I was mainly angry with you. But I did that night,
when I watched you walk, not even glancing at me. I did not
dream, however, that it would be thus."

"Nor did I."

"Are you ready now for the second proof?"

"Oh, but I am! Will you teach me the American ways?"

She turned on her side and drew me to her.

Day was breaking when I went to my room.

I slept until noon. On my way down to lunch I knocked at
her door. No answer. It was locked. She was not in the dining
room. I worked in the sunroom without the torment of the
day before.

At four o'clock I heard the latch click as someone entered
the garden gate. I knew that it was Madeleine. The door opened
and there she stood, breathing hard, her face troubled. I moved
to embrace her but she held me off.

"Oh my dear," she said, "a terrible thing has happened. My
sister's friend committed suicide this morning. I can tell you

no more now. I must return immediately."

My heart stopped. "To Paris?"

"To La Pinède, where my sister is. I ran all the way only to tell you where I am and that I cannot see you tonight."

"Can I be of help?"

"Friends have come from Nice. I must return now. Au revoir." She kissed me and left.

I read the story of the tragedy that evening in the *Éclaireur*. It was an affair of Lesbianism. The sister's "friend" was an "amie." Madeleine had come from Paris in an effort to dissuade her younger sister from further relations with an older Frenchwoman, a dilettante who had seduced the girl and brought her to the Riviera. Madeleine had apparently succeeded in persuading her sister to break away and accompany her back to Paris. Whereupon the chagrined Lesbian superficially wounded the girl, then shot herself successively through both heart and temple, a feat which the newspaper termed, "tout à fait miraculeux."

Madeleine did not return to Le Soleil that night nor for breakfast the next morning. As I was walking to the café toward noon, a Renault sedan overtook me. A handkerchief fluttered at the window. It was Madeleine, and a young woman and two men I had never seen before. I feared that she had had to leave without our meeting again. I worked all afternoon in blind concentration.

I went to my room after dinner and read in the only souvenir I had of her—a volume of François Mauriac's poems called *Orages* which she had loaned me. They were bittersweet poems of love won and love lost and of the burden carried by a sensual man. They spoke to me with a voice I had never heard in poetry. I read them now with new intensity and deeper meaning.

At last I turned out the lamp and went on my balcony. There was diminished light from the gibbous moon. No boats were on the water. The lighthouses of Ferrat and Antibes wheeled and stabbed. I ached for Madeleine. Had I lost her?

I lay down on my bed and must have dozed.

I was roused sometime later by a soft knocking on the door.

"Who is it?"

"C'est moi, Madeleine."

It was she, in coat, hat, and veil, beautiful and melting. I held her close and she put her cheek against mine.

"I need you, my love, Oh how I need you!" she murmured.

"You have me."

"I feared you would not be here. Your window was dark and there was no light under your door."

"I thought it was good-bye you waved this noon."

"So much has happened. You read in the paper, yes? You know then. It is ended. I put her on the Blue Train before they could detain her for an inquest, then I came to you as soon as I was able, my American lover."

"Who were those men in the car?"

"Only my cousins from Nice. You were jealous?"

"I have had gloomy thoughts. Now you have turned them golden."

"Don't put on the light. I must look like a witch. Let me go and bathe. Will you come then? The night is yours."

It was a beautiful night. Madeleine had seen the body of the dead Lesbian—the first corpse she had ever viewed—and in response to her sister's wish had helped wash and dress it for burial. The effect had been to turn her back toward life, so that I found her needful of my living body, her desire heightened to an almost unbearable ecstasy. We strove with all our might to perpetuate the life in us.

I awoke at daybreak and again slipped away to my own bed.

She rested in her room for the next twenty-four hours, then on the morning of the second day we went on an outing. I had read in the *Éclaireur* that the Italian liner "Rex," Genoa for New York, was due to call at Villefranche for passengers. We planned to be there when she put into the bay. They packed a lunch for us, and we set out by autobus to Nice, where we transferred to the Mentone bus.

Villefranche clings to the ankle of the Grande Corniche, a few miles east of Nice, its tall stucco houses forming a pastel conglomeration against the gray cliffs, two shades of green being supplied by terraced stands of olive and pine. The long finger of bay points seaward, bounded on each side by a narrow wooded cape.

We left the bus where the highway crosses the neck of the western cape, then followed a dirt road through pines on the crest until we had nearly reached the end of the cape. There we turned off and found a vantage point on the steep eastern slope. The blue bay was below us, its water unruffled under a windless sky. We were in a clearing among the pines, the ground carpeted with dead needles, the air fragrant with resin. I twitched a branch and a shower of pollen sifted down like yellow dust.

Madeleine lay on her back on the bed of needles. She wore a slack suit of fine-ribbed green corduroy, espadrilles on her bare feet. It was the first time I had seen her in casual clothes. I leaned on my elbow and watched the small boats coming in and out of the narrow bay.

"I brought your book," I said, reaching in my shirt and removing the little volume. "Do you know Mauriac? I mean, know him personally?"

"I do. He is a man of great feeling and kindness. He has been very good to me with the tenderness that comes to a few older men who have lived deeply sensual lives."

"His poetry expresses much suffering."

"It is from the struggle between soul and senses. It is obvious that he is an ardent Catholic. I trust you did not overlook the book's motto: *les derniers grondements d'une jeunesse que s'éloigne.* How does one say that in English?"

"One doesn't, at least not literally. I believe I know what it means."

"So do I! Oh Jean, my friend, it is more and more meaningful as my own youth recedes."

"Dare I ask your age, O ageless one?"

She laughed. "You express yourself so nicely. I really believe you should remain in France and enrich our culture."

"You tease me."

"Indeed I do not. I am a serious woman."

"Of what age?"

"You have been persistent almost from the first when, you will recall, you rejected my overture. But why do you need to ask my age, you who can take a woman's pulse without even touching her?"

"Thirty?"

"Oh thank you, you are truly a friend, but alas, you must add six."

"Such antiquity! All of eight years my senior. Soon we'll *both* be in our thirties."

"You will age well. You have learned good things."

"The most from you, my Madeleine."

At eleven o'clock, precisely on schedule, the bow of the "Rex" appeared from behind the eastern cape. She entered the bay and dropped anchor abreast of us, her twin black funnels banded with the Italian colors, a red and white house flag flying from her afterpeak. Steam rose from the fore-funnel, followed by a deep blast that was hurled back by the cliff.

We sat with drawn-up knees and watched a lighter with passengers and baggage approach and disgorge into the ship. Then she backed out of the bay and disappeared behind the western cape.

"Do you wish you were on board?" she asked.

"If you were with me."

"Are you never homesick?"

"Only lovesick."

I kissed her, but after a brief surrender, she freed herself.

"No you don't, Mr. Mellors. Morning in the open air is not a proper place."

"We could go beneath the pines where no eye would see us."

"The needles would hurt my flesh, and besides my ensemble is not fashioned for such an act."

"I am nevertheless very happy."

"You have been in love before."

"Never like this. You are a kind of incarnation of all the women I have ever known."

"You are an incorrigible flatterer. Are you not hungry? I die of hunger, being unaccustomed to such a vigorous life."

We lunched on bread and cheese and meat, and there was a wicker-covered bottle of chianti. The wine made us glow and she let me love her a little and gently, but mostly she wanted to talk.

"Ah, but you're a city girl," I said, bending over her. "The wonder is you are so healthy with no outdoor life at all. Everything about you is perfection: skin, hair, teeth."

"I have never been made love to so clinically. I like it. Tell me though, how long before I fade?"

"Never, if you follow my prescription of the other night. One golden bloom in wine taken with the evening meal. It would be best if I could prepare it for you."

"But you will be returning to your country."

"Not until summer. Come with me to Italy, to the villa near Florence where Lawrence wrote the book. Let us honeymoon there."

"Do not torment me, I beg of you. It is a miracle that I am here now."

"Where should you be?"

"In Paris, of course. Imagine how difficult it was to send my sister back alone. Our cousins were angry with me. I can tell you now. 'For that beachcomber?' they asked, when I pointed you out as we drove by. I was furious that they saw only the worn clothes and not you. It was then that I decided to stay."

"Did you see more than old clothes that first afternoon?"

"I saw your thin face, your wiry frame, your brown hands, and, oh, the way you selected the small stones and most delicately rubbed them clean before putting them in the sling. The grace of your movements. It was a marine tableau, a poem of utmost charm. I was drawn to you in spite of my wish to remain aloof, and that is why I spoke to you. Only to be ignored. Ah God, I blushed and would not raise my eyes to you that night."

"Why did you wish to remain aloof?"

"I wanted only to free my sister. I did not want a love affair. I am not a green girl, you know, in search of experience."

"Are you married?"

"Do not catechize me."

"Why did you let me love you?"

"I could not help it. I sought to remain impersonal, but in vain. You provoked in me exquisite feelings that I thought myself no longer capable of; and when I perceived that you are an artist, as well as a scientist, and that you know something of the way women are and would not be foolish or clumsy, then I gave myself to you with all my heart."

"But you won't out of doors."

"It would not be successful here."

"You French are more cold-blooded than we are."

"And wiser. You have lived among my people and our blood is in you so that you are not alien to me. You and your ways are a seductive blend of the familiar and the strange. How could I resist you?"

"You will come with me?"

"You must not ask that. It is not fair, for I cannot. I must return to Paris."

"When?"

"Tomorrow."

"Tomorrow?"

"I had not meant to tell you until tonight when you were leaving me. I must take the Blue Train."

"Then this is the last time."

"We have all day, all night."

I lay face down on the prickly needles and sought to hold back tears of chagrin. I felt unable to match her resignation.

"I did not want to love you either," I said finally. "For long I did not touch a woman, even a handclasp, but gave myself utterly to my work. The Cros was like Eden, without Eve."

"It was unnatural for you to remain chaste so long."

"You are so utterly French."

"What else, my love, what else would you have me?"

"I will always be hungry for you. Can we be together in Paris? I shall be there en route from Italy to England."

"When lovers part they can never come together again the same two persons. Time alters them. Time and distance. Who knows what they will do to us? There will be war again. There is always the fear of the Germans, the modern barbarians. The paper I work for is international in outlook and policy, but in my heart I do not believe. I fear."

"You are too fatalistic."

"Life has taught me to be."

"I have yet to learn."

"You must learn to take all when the time is ripe, as ours was. You must never forget the nature of idylls. They bud, they bloom, they fade."

"You leave even before ours is through blooming."

"That is our fate. I would have you think of this enchanted coast and those who have loved here before us. Phoenicians, Greeks and Romans, the barbarians, Italians, French. And now we two, Jean and Madeleine. Think of us, my love, as two of the brightest links in the long chain."

We dozed, side by side on the pine needles under the blue sky and golden showers of pollen.

Twilight found us back in Nice at the Café Monod on the Place Masséna, where English tea and Sandeman's port engendered more talk.

"There is no point in a man enjoying women," she said, "if he does not learn to apply to the next all that he has learned from the ones before. You did not come to me a gauche shepherd. You brought things learned from those you have told me of, all of them, even Nancy. And do you know the greatest thing a man or a woman can learn?"

"Tell me."

"That it is more satisfying to give pleasure than to receive it. But you do know this. We both do. That is why we are so good together."

"But after tonight you will stop giving."

"Then it is your turn, to give me the freedom to go. What if I had gone day before yesterday, as every reasonable impulse told me to do?"

"I shall never forget your coming to my darkened room."

"It was a supreme moment for me as well."

"Tell me how it is that you are beautiful and not vain or selfish?"

"I was once both."

"What can I hope for in a woman after you?"

"Your new wisdom and strength will attract good women. Like unto like. You must marry and father children."

"You have borne children?"

"Yes."

"That is why you are tender with me."

"Oui, mon enfant."

"One more?"

"Perhaps. It would be truly a love-child."

We walked across the Place to the Cagnes autobus stand, seeing the electric signs on the buildings—Aux Galeries Lafayette de Paris; L'Eté à Aix-les-Bains; Hotel Ruhl et des Anglais; Nestlé, Trésor des Mamans; Ostende, Belgique, Reine des Plages; Voyages en Italie—all the glittering signs, casting their light down on us.

We ate dinner at her table, and in honor of her departure, Monsieur Torquet opened an old bottle of St. Emilion. She was gay and adorable, and I loved her joyfully, hopelessly.

We went at once to her room after we had eaten, and undressed; and not wanting to make love in the dark, we dimmed the lamp with her red scarf. I remember that sometime toward morning she leaned over me and stroked my closed eyelids and whispered, "When you see me no longer, remember how I caressed your face." She lay back down and said, even softer, "Soon I will be old. And you as well, my love. How beautiful life is, how sad!"

I slept again until noon. She left a farewell note under my door. "I shall look for you when the Blue Train passes." There was also a sprig of lavender from a bouquet I had brought her.

Toward evening I leaned once again on the barrier and waited for the Blue Train to pass. It came with a shriek and a rush; and it went, leaving the dying sound of its wheels and the acrid smell of coal smoke. Was it she I saw at the window, waving? I could not be sure, so swift was the passage of the train.

The old man crept out to raise the barrier. This time I did not linger to talk with him.

V

Martha

My life at Le Soleil ended with the departure of Madeleine. I bought an excursion ticket to Italy that allowed stopovers in any city. Florence was the only one where I stayed a while, and there it was to visit the Villa Mirenda at Scandicci in the nearby countryside, where I sought vestiges of Lawrence's residence. From Rome I went to Naples and there obtained passage on a Dutch freighter to Rotterdam. A slow voyage with calls at Marseilles, Barcelona, and Casablanca saw my book finished, and I arrived midsummer in London with free time and a little money left.

I bought a Royal Mail freighter passage to California via Panama Canal three weeks hence, then settled into a Bloomsbury boardinghouse and passed the days in galleries, museums, libraries, and parks, and in the reading room of the Royal College of Physicians, examining the earliest editions of Vesalius and Paré, rare books that were never made available by French libraries to mere students.

The time was early summer, the weather fair, tourists few. The Depression cut deeply into foreign travel. London was sedate after Paris and Rome. It was my first visit to the British capital and I liked it more than I thought I would, responding to the sober English character, the friendliness of the people in the streets, and their sense of self-reliance and certainty.

I sought to understand what Madeleine had given me. I felt mature at last and ready for whatever life held for me. As for loving another woman, I could not conceive of one to match the gifts of the Frenchwoman I had known so briefly and yet with such powerful effect. Besides, the English women were unalluring.

Then one morning at the American Express I found a letter from my cousin Robert, the son of my mother's sister, a coffee and tea importer in San Francisco, which read in part:

"Dear Jack, Mother gave me your travel letter saying you

106

will be in London for a few weeks, and I hasten to ask you to be nice to my fiancée Martha Cameron. She'll be there about the same time as you with her mother on her way back from Munich. I wanted her to get married a year ago, but she insisted on going, and now she's due back and we'll get married in Piedmont. I hope you'll be back for it. Business is very good for us in spite of the Depression—you know how people like their morning drink—and if you wanted to go into business I sure could make you a lot of money in this operation. Enclosed is a twenty for you and her to take in a show or two, and if there's any left over, bring me a Dunhill pipe, the kind with a short straight stem and a medium bowl. Be good to Martha but not too good.
Yours, Bob."

His letter was followed a day later by a note from Martha Cameron, giving her London hotel address. It was another few days before I overcame inertia and wrote, suggesting a rendezvous at the American Express office in the Haymarket; and it was there in the lobby that we met in mutual appraisal.

"So you are Bob's cousin Jack!"

"At your service, Miss Cameron."

"Out of a sense of duty."

"And curiosity."

"How do I look?"

"Cool."

"Do you really like it? I got it in Prague."

She was wearing a coarse linen skirt and a white blouse embroidered with red and blue flowers, and sandals on her bare feet.

"They say it's going to be another hot day. You are sensible to dress this way."

"Where are we going?"

"Lyon's Corner House. Do you mind eating there?"

We walked to the top of the Haymarket to the restaurant around the corner, and there we were seated at a marble-topped table in a quiet corner.

She was not pretty. Her eyes were small and close set, but a clear blue. Her nose was too large for her freckled face, her hair sand color. Her mouth was her best feature, wide and generous, the lower lip full, almost bee-stung. Her hands, as they played nervously with the silver before we were served chilled salads, toast and tea, were long fingered and blue veined. Her bare arms were white and also freckled. She was as tall as I, with shapely legs and feet. Her breasts swelled the flowered blouse.

"Well," she said. "Do you like what you see?"

"I can't decide whether you're a farm or a chorus girl."

She laughed. "I *was* born in the country, but on a vineyard, not a farm."

"Where did you meet Bob?"

"At Cal."

"I suppose you have been studying German business methods."

"Heavens no."

"What then?"

"Art."

"Art?"

"Why do you look astonished?"

"I can't imagine Bob . . ."

"I know. You think he's a Philistine. He is."

"Why are you marrying him?"

"Aren't you being rather personal, Dr. Burgoyne?"

"How would you like me to be?"

"Yourself."

"All right then, why are you marrying him?"

"He loves me."

"And you don't love him?"

"I didn't say I didn't."

"He and I are not alike."

"What are you like?"

"I like painting. Do you paint?"

"I try."

"Have you been to the Tate?"

"I haven't been anywhere in London. Mother is a hypochondriac. I've been devoting myself to her."

"When is the marriage?"

"This fall. Will you come?"

"If I get an appointment in the Bay region."

"Bob says you're a brain."

"I also have an organ called the heart."

"Tell me about its beat."

"Regular."

"I expected to find you terribly intellectual. You're really quite . . ."

"Ordinary."

"Entertaining is what I was going to say."

"I said I was at your service."

"It's a relief to be with an American man."

"Are Germans on the make?"

"They think art students are to bed down."

"Well?"

"I'm really a Puritan."

"All but your mouth."

"What do you mean?"

"It was made for kissing."

"I promised Bob I'd wait till we were married."

"Haven't you ever?"

"With him, naturally, but not with anyone else."

She put down her fork and took a swallow of tea and leaned forward on her elbows. "The marble feels cool, doesn't it. You're not an M.D., I know, but you have studied and know a lot."

"And lived a bit."

"I need to talk to someone."

"I'm here. What about?"

"Bob."

"Yes?"

"He can never make love to me without drinking a lot first."

"It sounds like he is the Puritan. There are many fetishes some find necessary before they can have intercourse."

"I'd like to think I'm fetish enough."

"I'd say you are."

She laughed. "I confess to loving it, fetish and all."

"The year must have been a long one to go without."

"Long in every way. I've had time to think."

"About marrying Bob?"

"About everything. I'm glad you'll let me unburden."

"Bob's a money-maker. And you'll never be out of tea and coffee."

She laughed again. "I've grown up with money. Dad owns the Beau Soleil winery and lots of other things. This year I've learned other values."

"My grandfather owned a vineyard. I went to see it in Auxerre. It's still there."

"Was he rich?"

"He had just enough vines to make his own wine. They say he regretted emigrating, but he made money in a San Diego real estate boom, and my father became a doctor, and here I am."

"I'm uncertain."

"Then why do it?"

"It's gone so far. The families have it all settled, especially what *they're* going to wear. Besides, I don't want to hurt Bob."

"Why not stay away another year? He'll wait, won't he?"

"I haven't any talent."

"We all have uncertainties."

"Is studying all you've done?"

"The first year. Since then I have had some interruptions."

"Interesting ones?"

"Educational ones. I'm not the same as when I first arrived in Europe."

"Women?"

"Women."

"I can listen."

"Let's walk. It would be too long a story."

I went with her along Piccadilly as far as Fortnum and Mason's where she was to meet her mother. I believed that this would be our only meeting; and then, as we were saying good-bye, something made me ask, almost against my will,

"Would you like to see the Tate?"

"With you?"

"Who else?"

"I thought maybe you were arranging a tour for lonely women."

"Meet me at Amexco again tomorrow at eleven."

"It sounds lovely."

That evening I dithered. I did not want an affair involving my cousin. I went so far as to draft a telegram saying I had been called away. It sounded flimsy. I tore it up. I went to sleep dreaming of Martha's lower lip.

We met on another hot morning, and Martha was again dressed in cool linen with bare legs and sandaled feet, like a flower amidst the wilted tourist throng, her homely face lit and friendly, as we came together in the crowded lobby. My inertia vanished as I realized that I, too, was lonely for someone from home.

We walked to the bottom of the Haymarket and boarded a Number 32 bus, climbed to the top and sat behind the windscreen as the red monster rolled through Trafalgar Square, down Whitehall, past Westminster Abbey, and along Millbank to the riverside Tate Gallery, its Portland stone a dirty gray from London's grime.

The interior was cool and colorful. We wandered through rooms of Turners, the pre-Raphaelites, and contemporary British painters, pausing before Stanley Spencer's fantastic "Resurrection," coming at last to the rooms of the French Impressionists. There Martha's grip on my arm tightened and I felt her response as we walked past the glowing walls of Renoir nudes, Gauguin's tawny Tahitians, the golden checkerboards and blue mountains of Cezanne's Provençal landscapes, Vincent's grain fields and wind-blown cypresses and little yellow chair, the ballet girls and beer drinkers of Dégas, and last of all, a Monet painting of blue poplars against white clouds.

Now Martha was pressed against me, her body like a harp under the touches of form and color. Thus had Erda responded to music. I knew that we were moving toward denouement. We did not speak. Painting was our tongue.

We stopped on the way out to look at the sculpture in the foyer—a stone woman with crushed lips and breasts by

Gaudier-Brjeska called "Chanteuse Triste;" a crucifixion and an Eve by Eric Gill, demonstrating his twin loves for the religious and the erotic; Rodin's "Fallen Caryatid" and his head of Balzac.

When I saw that she liked these last pieces, I suggested that we go next to the Victoria and Albert Museum and see the collection of sculptures given by Rodin during the World War.

"We haven't eaten," I reminded her.

"You have fed me."

And so we walked hand in hand along the Embankment in the shade of the plane trees, seeing the Thames with its traffic of tugs and barges.

I asked directions of a bobby at the Albert Bridge, and then we boarded the bus that took us via the Marble Arch and Kensington to the Victoria and Albert. There we spent an hour in the cool dark rooms of the Museum where sunlight never reached, looking at the Rodins and the replicas of Florentine bronzes by Donatello and Giambologna. Martha paused in front of Rodin's "Fallen Angel," a bronze of two women in an intertwined position, their mouths joined, one woman on her back, bent like a bow.

"I am not sure that I like it," she said.

I ran my hands over the cold metal. "He was a bull of a man. I can see him tearing the two apart and making love to them separately."

"It's a wonder the English would allow it."

"The title puts them off. They think it's something from Milton."

She laughed.

We left the museum and crossed to Hyde Park and lay on the grass in the shade of great poplars. People drifted around us, dogs played, and in the distance the buses honked like geese.

"My feet are hot," Martha said.

"Let me unbuckle your sandals."

I held her bare foot in my hands and massaged it gently, then the other. She lay back and closed her eyes.

"It's lovely," she murmured.

"The feet are generally neglected. Men think hands are the only things worth holding."

"I never knew I could feel close to someone so quickly."

"Art does it."

"I'm glad you're not on the make."

"I thought maybe I was."

"Well, not obviously."

"There are other ways to make love than pushing a woman down on her back."

"How did you know the way to a woman's heart is through her feet?"

"A footnote in Gray's *Anatomy*."

She laughed. "Bob would think we're crazy."

"Art intoxicates."

"Art and Jack. I hate not being a good painter."

"Being a good woman comes first."

"What is good?"

"Said jesting Cameron and would not stay for an answer."

"I like you."

"And I you."

"I'm leaving tomorrow night."

"A good thing, too."

"Don't you want me to stay?"

"What would we do?"

"Man leads, woman follows."

"Your hands remind me of Rossetti's *Silent Noon*. 'Your hands lie open in the long fresh grass, the finger points shine through like rosy blooms.' "

"Why didn't you find me in Munich?"

"Je ne sprache pas Deutsch."

"It was a wasted year."

"You'd better marry Bob soon, if you're going to."

"Mother wonders why I toss and turn at night. I can't talk to her, she's such a prude. She told me once her husband had never seen her naked. I hate what she did to him. He was once a virile man, I know. Now he's her eunuch. She said she wouldn't sleep in the same room with me if I didn't wear a nightgown."

"You sleep naked?"

"Don't you?"

"In weather like this."

"Bob's a prude, too."

"I don't know him at all. I already know you much better."

"We met only yesterday. It didn't take long, did it?"

"I know that the relationship between a man and a woman, the physical act, can be the most beautiful thing on earth. Not automatically and not always. Rarely, I guess. But then it can be so intense and creative as to make all the forms of art which flow from it mere echoes and reflections."

"You speak with conviction."

"Being in Europe has taught me everything."

"Tell me some you've learned."

"I can't tell it. I can only be it."

"I think I know what you mean."

The hot afternoon passed and we had neither lunch nor tea. We lay on the grass and talked and were silent, talked more and then dozed, in "a close-companioned inarticulate hour, when twofold silence was the song of love."

"Can we have supper together?" I asked, as we finally rose to leave.

"Mother has theater tickets. Dine with us at the hotel. Mother would like to meet you."

"Would I like mother?"

"No." She took my hand. "But you like me; you said you did."

"I do. You lead now and I'll follow."

We walked through Kensington Gardens, past the duck pond, the statue of Peter Pan and the sunken garden, to her hotel.

Mrs. Cameron was a reserved woman. I could strike no sparks from her, and we were able to converse at all only when I steered the talk to the subject of her own health.

Then we were saying good-bye in the lobby and again Martha's widened eyes spoke to me, and I heard myself asking her to dine with me the following evening.

"I'm sorry," Mrs. Cameron replied, "tomorrow is our last day. We are going to Hampton Court and won't be back until late. Our boat train leaves at one a.m. Something about the *Mauretania* sailing with the tide. Martha couldn't possibly see you again, Dr. Burgoyne."

She held out her hand. I ignored it and looked at Martha. She had blanched so that the freckles were jumping off her face. She looked at her mother, then at me. The denouement still lay ahead. I would not be denied.

"What time will you be back?" I asked Martha.

"By six."

"Meet me in front of Selfridge's at seven-thirty. I know a French restaurant you'll love. And there's Duke Ellington at the Palladium. I'll get you to the boat train on time. Your mother can take the bags in a cab. After all, Bob asked *me* to look after you in London."

Mrs. Cameron was speechless.

"I'm going to do it, mother. I'm not going to sit around this hotel until midnight."

Mrs. Cameron turned her back and went to the lift. Martha seized my hand. Her eyes were enormous.

"Thank God! I would have backed down."

"Pour Robert et pour la patrie. Do you want to see me a last time?"

She squeezed my hand. "Guess."

The next day seemed endless. I tried to bury the thought of Martha, the coolness of her garb, her fair freckled skin, widened eyes and bee-stung lip and the feel of her naked feet in my hand, but her image burned in me like a live coal.

Yet I made no plans. How could I? I had little money and less time. I sought to pass the day by walking, clear to St. Paul's, and there with a guide up onto the catwalk around the base of the dome from where we could see for miles around.

I returned to my lodging for tea and cucumber sandwiches, shaved again, took a bath and donned fresh clothes, and was waiting in front of Selfridge's in Oxford Street when Martha stepped off the bus. She was wearing a gray woolen skirt and a short-sleeved purple cashmere pullover, sandals on her bare feet. Her expectant face was lovely to see.

"Not too tired?" I asked.

"Oh Jack, why did you wait until the very last minute to ask me? Didn't you know I was praying all through dinner for you to ask me out my last night in London?"

"Is your mother still angry?"

"I shouldn't tell you this, but coming back on the boat, do you know what she said? She said she would be happier if I were marrying someone more mature than Bob. Someone like Dr. Burgoyne."

"You made that up."

"You buffaloed her."

"What did you say?"

"I said I didn't know anyone like Dr. Burgoyne."

"You'll be happy with Bob once you're married."

"He cabled that he's meeting the boat in New York."

"Don't give up your painting."

"When do you leave?"

"Next Thursday on the *Loch Clair*. It takes a whole month to San Pedro."

"I wish, I wish . . ."

"Dreamer."

We walked through Oxford Circus and on to Bloomsbury and the French restaurant in Charlotte Street called "Chez Antoine." There we sat at one of four candle-lit tables on the privet-hedged *terrasse*, and after plates of leek and potato soup, we ate cold roast beef, sliced cucumbers and tomatoes and French bread, and drank a bottle of chilled vin rosé. The garçon was pleased by the relish with which we dispatched the food.

"You're a healthy one," I observed, as we finished with coffee and cognac.

"Witty, not pretty."

"More beautiful each time."

"It's you."

"It was a long day."

"You wanted me to come."

"I wanted nothing else."

"You seem so serene about everything."

"I wasn't today. I could hardly wait for you to come down river. Now the time will pass too fast. What shall we do?"

"What *can* we do?"

"The Duke's at the Palladium. Want to go?"

"Do you?"

"I want what you want."

"Then can't we just talk? Maybe walk somewhere?"

"How did you know that's what I really want to do?"

"You make me feel that we're doing what I want to do, and yet I know that it's you who's leading. You know what a woman wants."

"What does a woman want?"

"Strength that's gentle."

"I didn't always know it."

"Live and learn."

"Live and love."

"I'm afraid it's too late."

It was nearly ten o'clock by the time we had finished the coffee and a second cognac. It was still twilight. The moon had risen from behind the row of high dwellings across the narrow street. Antoine came out for a breath of air. When he greeted us in French, I replied in his tongue.

"I thought you were French," he said, "but I cannot determine your region."

"California."

"But that is in America."

"I am American, but my paternal grandfather was French. He lived in Auxerre and made his own wine. Mademoiselle's father lives in California and makes his own wine. She and I drink the wine that others make."

"You have both the form and the spirit of a Frenchman. You are also an artist."

"I am a scientist. Mademoiselle is the artist. She is a painter."

"Many painters live in Charlotte Street. Your Whistler had his studio across from us. What does Mademoiselle paint?"

"He wants to know what you paint," I said to her in English.

"I am old-fashioned enough," she replied, "to believe that the human body is the best subject."

"But of course," Antoine agreed, "providing it is unclothed."

"We need your counsel, patron," I said. "Mademoiselle's boat train departs at one a.m., alas, and before then she wishes to take a walk. For exercise, that is, having eaten this enormous meal. And, I hasten to add, I intend to accompany her, although I ate much more abstemiously."

"Great liar," she said, ruffling my hair.

"She is far too precious and tender a creature," I continued, "to be turned loose in London on a night like this. Can you, will you, patron, in fact, you must recommend a likely promenade."

"No sidewalks or pavements," Martha said. "Remember, I'm a country girl from Calistoga."

"It is true, patron," I said. "This delicate slip of a thing was actually born and raised in a vineyard. For all I know, she was conceived in one."

"How charming," Antoine exclaimed, in English. "How utterly charming. Let me offer a liqueur in the nymph's honor."

"More cognac," Martha growled.

"Three for the road," Antoine roared.

We toasted exuberantly and then Antoine said, "I know the perfect promenade for you two nature-lovers. You are probably aware that London's parks close at nightfall—all but one. Do you know where Primrose Hill is? The other side of Regents Park, not far from the Zoo."

"I love monkeys," Martha said.

"Be serious," Antoine chided, "and hear me out. The Hill is London's only unfenced park. One can walk there all the night long."

"But we haven't all night," I said.

"How far is it?" Martha asked.

"Go to Russell Square and take a 169. It will set you down at the foot of the hill. In this prolonged drought, which I just heard on the news is due momentarily to break; in this dry weather the grass will be likewise."

"I beg your pardon, patron," I said, "It should be emphasized that we are friends, not lovers."

Antoine peered at us, then smiled. "It is better to be friends first and lovers afterward, than the other way around."

"You are a philosopher," Martha said.

"I am a Frenchman," Antoine replied, "which is the same thing."

I paid the bill and we set out for Russell Square. The bus came soon and in another twenty minutes we were at the foot of Primrose Hill. We walked arm in arm up the path to the top of the low hill, turned, and saw London far and wide beneath us. The sounds of traffic were muted. The moon was orange colored through the warm air.

"What time is it?" Martha asked.

"Eleven-fifteen."

"Can you keep track? I can't."

"Trust me to."

"I do, oh I do."

"This is our last time."

"I know."

"I'll surely see you again, but it won't be the same, with you Bob's wife."

"I know everything tonight. Remy Martin makes me clairvoyant."

"I'm a wee bit drunk," I confessed.

We walked on over the crest and off the path onto the grass. I reached down and felt it.

"Antoine was right. It's as dry as my mouth."

I took her arm and pulled her gently.

"Sit down here. It won't stain your skirt."

"What's a mere skirt on a night like this?"

She stretched out on her back, arms at her side, and stared at me. I sat down beside her. A faint breeze rustled the may trees. Crickets sang and we heard the sounds of switch engines, shunted cars, and an occasional whistle from a nearby railway yard. The dry grass filled the air with sweetness. I looked down at Martha. She smiled up at me. I lay down beside her. There were no words.

My hand was paralyzed. Only by enormous effort did I

force it to find her bare arm with my fingertips.

"How cool your skin is!"

"Is it as cool as that marble you touched?"

"No, there's fire beneath the skin."

For answer her hand found mine and our fingers joined and began to woo "with the hot blood's blindfold art." I slid my hand beneath her sweater. Her breasts were bare. She began to tremble.

"No," she whispered, rolling free. "It's all or none."

I got up and walked behind a may tree and made water.

When I returned, she had turned on her belly. Again I sat beside her, and now I began to caress the length of her curved body, then gently turned her over and found her lips with mine. Ours was a deep, searching kiss.

She finally broke away. "If you do," she said, "I'll never leave you."

"Good," I said. "I'll never let you go."

I drew her roughly to me and again we kissed with hungry relief. We had gone over the falls. I had no power to stop, no thought of anything but the gift of her body, now open, arched and ready, the flesh on fire, burning, burning.

Then I heard a cough nearby. I started up. There at a respectful distance stood two helmeted bobbies. I waited, thinking they would move along. They did not. I helped Martha to her feet and we adjusted our clothes. The bobbies saluted and went on and took position at a respectful distance.

We walked back down the hill. In the arc light at the foot I dared look at my watch. Twelve-fifteen. We ran along Park Row until we reached the cab rank. A single vehicle was there. I spoke to the venerable driver.

"Waterloo Station. A one o'clock boat train. Can you make it?"

"With minutes to spare, sir," was the confident reply, and away we chugged through the quiet streets.

Martha lay in my arms and we kissed. Her face was wet with tears.

"Because I'm happy," she said when I sought to comfort her. "It was decided for us."

"There was no virtue in me," I said.

"I was yours, all yours."

"You've kept your promise to Bob."

"Hold me, darling, all the way. You don't feel cheated?"

"A thousand times no. It was more wonderful than any loving I've ever known."

"Remember, when you see us go down the aisle."

"Darling, darling, my beautiful darling!"

We reached Waterloo Station at quarter to one. I tipped the driver half a crown and we rushed through the swarming station to the boat-train gate. There Mrs. Cameron fell on us with a cry of relief.

"I told you I would," I said. "Here's your darling daughter and all in one piece."

"God knows what you two have been up to," she said. "Martha's hair is a fright. And is that grass on her skirt?"

"Dry grass," Martha laughed, as we ran along the platform to Mrs. Cameron's compartment.

We boarded with minutes to spare, then Martha walked back to the vestibule with me and we kissed good-bye with hunger and tenderness in our touch.

Back on the platform I stood beneath their compartment. Martha put down the window and reached her hand to me. Her face was transfigured. Her lips kept soundlessly saying my name. The train began to move. I walked along still holding her hand, until we were pulled apart.

I watched the Southampton Express go by, its cream and red cars bearing the Cunard arms on their sides. Swift and swifter and then gone and the coal smoke drifting back. For the first time I felt cold sober.

I walked across Waterloo Bridge to Piccadilly and the all-night Lyons Corner House, and here I took the same table where we had lunched so long ago, only two days ago. I laid my hands palm down on the cold marble, and when the waitress came for my order, I said, "All I want, please, is a bowl of bread and milk."

"I say, that's sensible. You'll sleep well, sir. I always take one at the end of my day."

"It was beginning to rain as I came in."

"Pshaw, we planned a Sunday picnic. Now the grass will be wet."

"You should have gone tonight. The grass was dry."

She looked closely at me. "Are you from the country, sir?"

"Yes, I am. From Primrose Hill."

She laughed and went for my order.

AFTERWORD

in a letter to the author
from

HENRY MILLER

May 29, 1943
The Glen

Dear Larry,

I'm glad I had the chance to reread your book: it seems even better to me on second reading. For me it is the only book by an American which deals with *les amourettes*; it is also the first book by an American which gives to these little, passing loves the proper frame, the proper fragrance. It occupies a realm which is quite blank in our literature; it has a pagan, sophisticated quality which removes it from the sentimental or the immoral. It is thoroughly amoral—and aesthetic; its contour is spherical, finite and melodious. Each episode carries its own carnal glow; in each there is a blossoming, a ripening and a death. It is on the level of nature throughout, and it is this which gives one such a good feeling on putting the book down. It is true also that it is permeated with that melancholy which inspired the phrase—*la chair est triste*.

There are so many things about your book I like and admire that I scarcely know where to begin. Perhaps it has a special charm for me because of its European setting. Everything you refer to in your excursions and explorations, all your little observations, your discoveries and delights, I share intimately. In reading you I relive my own life abroad. With this difference—that I like your life better. I like what I must curiously call the "chaste" aspect. Behind the ardent lover there is always the serious student, and behind him the strange American that all of us are. For we are a strange species when set down in a foreign land. We are so awkward, so stupidly earnest, so childishly hungry, so inept, so inflexible. And yet we are loved, whenever we give the foreigner a chance to know us, to see into our hearts. And we are loved, and eventually respected, precisely for that quality which your Jack Burgoyne is always revealing—*tenderness*. That is the one thing we have to offer to the European woman. And it is something for which she seems to be perpetually craving.

In the episode which concerns Madeleine Montrechet, for me the peak of the book, I was shocked at first, and then suddenly thrilled, to find your hero reading to her from "Lady Chatterley's Lover." It was *her* book, I know, and perhaps that is why I read with such expectancy. What a strange figure this Mellors must have seemed to her! But what Mellors had was tenderness—and humor. No one has emphasized that enough, in studying this curious book of Lawrence's. It was the death-blow to the sickly English sentimentality which pervades their romances. And it is a humor unthinkable to a Mediterranean people, where carnal love is concerned. But, once again, I must compliment you on a little observation—which Madeleine makes when you take her to Villefranche to see the *Rex* lying at anchor in the bay. No love-making outdoors! It's unnatural! How French, that! And how right—for them. In the Lawrence book it was almost necessitous—to take Lady Chatterley outdoors and tumble her over. It was necessary to bring the pale, sickly English body out into the sunshine, to expose it to the light, to weld it to the sun-beaten earth which it had forgotten.

And while on this subject of Lawrence, how grateful I am to you for including the passage from "Apocalypse." How many times I have read that particular passage. Each phrase is burned into my memory. Nowhere in Lawrence is there anything to compare with this for truth and poignancy. It is as though he added something to the Bible, a coda concerning the flesh which had been overlooked by those who thought only of man's soul. "Man wants his physical fulfillment first and foremost, since now, once and once only, he is in the flesh and potent." What Lawrence forgot, in speaking of man's not wanting his own isolate salvation of his soul, is that in other times, other religions—I am thinking of India particularly—man did find salvation, fulfillment and God through love. The Hindus had their Bhakti Yoga as well as all the other forms of yoga. In Hindu lore the great love unions ended in bliss, in a sort of deification of flesh and spirit. In the West the great love sagas end in agony and death. But that, it seems to me, was always the fault of the man. He could not carry the woman through to the heavenly gates; he foundered in the sexual embrace.

But to return to specific delights . . . . This peculiar charm of the American abroad, which so many writers have treated of—Henry James at one pole and Mark Twain at the other—what a pleasure you give us in observing *l'education sentimentale* of Jack Burgoyne! Very wise of you to round it off with a quintet. Just as in the musical form, there is in these five episodes a true progression. There is a beginning which is harsh and strident and an end which is utterly harmonious in its unresolved fulfillment. The whole development reveals precisely what a book of this sort should reveal—mastery. Mastery in the art of love, I mean. It was absolutely fitting that the penultimate episode should revolve around the very womanly figure of Madeleine Montrechet. It was like an enriching and deepening of the second movement, with Erda. Two earth feelings—one of the cold North, one of the warm Mediterranean. Erda gives the body, but the soul is not yet awake. Madeleine warms the body with spirit. But with Madeleine, as one so often discovers in this region, there is always the thought of "decay," of the fading of powers and the loss of beauty. There is a scepticism born of the sun's fierce heat, a false knowledge of death, I might say. How accurate was your intuition in making those two references to death in this episode. Particularly the latter one, when she comes to you after washing the corpse! But the greatest delight which the book brings is the atmosphere that permeates it. A gentle, soothing atmosphere, even though it be the bleak winter of Dijon or the mean, rainy season of Paris. An atmosphere in which food and wines play an important role. Your cafés are especially redolent. Even the station buffets. And how wonderful it is to go with you to the station and watch the express or the "rapide" shoot by! In every chapter there are trains, it seems: always "le voyage," always "le depart." These night trains come and go, flash like meteors across the sky. Thank you for making the trains come alive! Beautiful objects they are; each time we take one they carry with them some precious part of us.

Yes, there are two atmospheres always—the one through which the story is moving and the other which accompanies it like a refrain, the one evoked by longing and desire, or by pain and remembrance. "The Morvan country lay to the west . . . ." You have no idea how enchanting it is to come upon such an observation. A few lines and we are webbed in Celtic magic and imagery. Or take your frequent little references to the names of those who once lived here—of Rameau making his music in Dijon, of Henry James penning the last lines of his book on a certain bench, of the two famous lovers who spent a night in an old house. Or the "flowery Chablis" which made the nostrils of the other diners expand with pleasure. Or the reference to Vézelay and her Romanesque basilica. Or the blonde Vézelise beer of Dijon. Or you go into the hills near Grasse and you remember to gather a large sachet of wild lavender which is then in bloom. Or you stand on the beach near Cagnes and sling pebbles. Or you return and find her standing against the mimosa, her face uplifted to the moon. And you say—"The still air was heavy with the mingled scent of mimosa, eucalyptus, rose-geranium and sea wrack." Sea wrack! How lucky to recall that! How disturbing and just! Or to think to remind us of "the limestone walls of the Ouche." Everything brings us back to the senses and to their importance not only in art but love. So that when we come to the Rodin figure it is indispensable that you caress it with your hands, as later you will caress the flanks of the one you are making love to. Always a "making love"—a making love "to" and "with." Is it not one of the first things we Americans learn on reaching France—the meaning of *faire l'amour*? A making and a doing—something plastically creative—not just a state of being, however intoxicating. How grateful we were to discover that every French lover is if not an artisan an artist, or vice versa. It is as though we discovered that in love we had existed without arms or legs, that in conversation we had never enjoyed the experience of using the hands, the fingers, to say nothing of the face muscles.

Yes, food and wine, excursions to *la campagne*—and books and music. In every situation there is an ambiance in which the total being participates. It is this perpetual ambiance—like a perpetual temperature—which makes these episodes anything but obscene in character. All of them pivot on sex, true. In all of them it is the taking of the citadel which is paramount, yet how unimportant that becomes if we but glance from the bed and take register of the opaque atmosphere in which all is swimming. How beautiful those little moments by the big window—all Dijon outside, a museum of statues and light, a city groaning with fine wines and with memories of a splendid past. You stand by the window inhaling the fragrance of the street and it is so infinitely more than anything the girl can ever possibly give, though she gave her soul. And how marvelous a mood you evoke when you say of one of your characters—the dipsomaniac—"Each night we did exactly the same things. Beer and talk at the Concorde, steak and red burgundy at the Pré-aux-Clercs, a bottle of mousseux in her room, love-making and sleep." Exactly the regimen for that sort of affair. It will go on and on; it will make no sense to others. And then one day it comes to an abrupt stop. The very repetitiousness is what is exciting. It is like striking the same chord again and again—and then presto! the mood is gone, there is an end—but the memory is hammered in, and when the memory of it returns it is the blood that beats, the blood that remembers.

Perhaps the clue to the beauty of this little book lies in your own words to Martha: "I do know that the physical relationship between a man and a woman can be the most

127

beautiful thing on earth. Simple and beautiful—sometimes. Not every time—just some times." To understand it fully we turn in our minds to some anterior epoch, to one of those periods when the adoration of woman, flowering from the myth of the Virgin, was coupled with a marriage between the male and the female minds. There was a period, we like to think, when Love was enthroned. A period when marriages were consummated first in Paradise, soul meeting soul, and then again the flesh. But the road to the fleshly union lay through the mind. A mind trying earnestly to recapture the flavor of the past. You express it quite beautifully yourself. "Perhaps we are like Paolo and Francesca. Dante tells how they were reading together in the garden one day, and when they came to a certain passage they turned and kissed. Then they laid aside the book and read no more that day." A little *aperçu* such as this speaks volumes. It is as if now, in our own time, walled up in some ugly prison, we catch through the bars of our oubliette a fleeting glimpse of love enacted with passion and faith and intelligence. Then love was a global trine and the consummation was complete in every realm—or failed utterly, so that even the earth was mired. A man or a woman's portrait was made against a magical landscape; the human being was an integral part of that landscape.

Well, Larry, I suppose I could go on indefinitely. Enough, however, to show you how much I appreciate what you have attempted. It is the sort of book I should like to present to those about to venture into the realm of love. A little handbook, a manual of love, to replace the ancient Kama Sutra which was meant to be instructive and not pornographic.

Henry